SCHOOLING THE ALIEN

BEASTLY ALIEN BOSS, BOOK 8

AVA ROSS

SCHOOLING THE ALIEN

Beastly Alien Boss, Book 8

Copyright © 2023 Ava Ross

All rights reserved.

No part of this book may be reproduced in any form or by any electronic or mechanical means, including information storage and retrieval systems, without written permission from the author, except for the use of brief quotations with prior approval. Names, characters, events, and incidents are a product of the author's imagination. Any resemblance to an actual person, living or dead is entirely coincidental.

Cover art by Natasha Snow Designs

Editing/Proofreading by JA Wren & Owl Eyes Proofs & Edits

FOREWORD

A note to the reader.

If you found this book outside of Amazon,
it's likely a stolen/pirated copy.
Authors make nothing when books are pirated.
If authors are not paid for their work,
they can't afford to keep writing.

SERIES BY AVA

Mail-Order Brides of Crakair

Brides of Driegon

Fated Mates of the Ferlaern Warriors

Fated Mates of the Xilan Warriors

Holiday with a Cu'zod Warrior

Galaxy Games

Alien Warrior Abandoned

Beastly Alien Boss

Bride of the Fae

A Sci-Fi Holiday Tail

Monsterville, USA

Monster on Board
(co-written with Alana Khan)

Third Galaxy on the Left

You can find my books on Amazon.

SCHOOLING THE ALIEN

Do I dare give my broken heart to an alien as wounded as me?

When I took a nanny job in a distant colony caring for two young boys who recently lost their mother, I expected I'd grow to love them. Having experienced loss myself, I knew how hard it was to heal. What I didn't expect was to fall for their father, a big, burly alien with scars on his body that mirrors those in my soul.

Between teaching the boys and bringing fun back into their lives, I get to know Firoh, a guy I sense needs love as much as me. It isn't long before I can see myself living in this alien colony forever as long as I can be with Firoh and his sons.

But when the boys' past threatens everything Firoh and I are building together, we'll have to expose our hearts to each other to fight off the threat.

Schooling the Alien is Book 8 and the final book in the Beastly Alien Boss Series. Each book is standalone, though loosely connected. They can be read in any order. Expect strong women and heroes who will do anything to be with their fated mates.

Trigger: the loss of a child in the main character's history, prior to the start of the book, and Firoh's sons have lost their mother. Readers do not experience this with the characters, though they refer to it and mourn.

1

MOLLY

Once my divorce was final, I packed my things. I stood in the front hall afterward, realizing how few possessions I had compared to Tyler. Only three boxes after ten years of marriage.

Plus one teardrop blue stone I wore strung on a simple chain about my neck, all I had left of the baby I'd lost before I could deliver her a year ago.

"I'll help you put them in your vehicle," Tyler said, his face stoic as always. I imagined it would loosen up after I'd left.

He left Bridgette's side, striding to the front door.

I did my best not to notice her softly bulging belly. He'd barely waited six months after I lost our daughter, Sara, before planting a new child in someone else.

"I can handle it," I said.

Since I had no place to go, he'd lived with Bridgette until I could "get my feet under me". Now that the divorce was final, however, I had to move out. The house and everything inside it legally belonged to my wealthy ex. Per our prenup, I got a small stipend that would be just enough to rent an apartment, though not enough to eat or buy myself a new pair of shoes.

It was okay. I could get a job.

Lifting a box, I propped it on my hip, then grabbed my bag of clothing. "You can get the door for me, Tyler. Maybe place the other boxes out on the stoop? I'll put these inside my hovercar," mine being a generous way to describe the rental, "then come back for the other two."

"Don't be like that," he snapped, "I'll take them to your hovercar."

So generous.

Bridgette released a shrill laugh, quickly cutting it off with a hand slapped over her mouth.

In the past, I would've strode right up to him, poked him in the chest, and told him I could be any way I pleased. Now, I just gave him one of those looks that made him squirm. I didn't have much else I could use to defend myself.

Outside, I shivered in the chilly winter air, taking care on the walk not to slip.

Tyler followed me with the final boxes stacked in his arms, leaving Bridgette inside the house. He opened the trunk of the small hovercar and lowered my few possessions inside. "What do you plan to do?"

"You know me. I always bounce back. I've got a new job lined up, and I'll start that soon."

I didn't add, *I'll forget I was ever with you.* Over the past six months, I'd already done most of the work of pushing him out of my heart and my life. I mourned the loss of our daughter more than I did our marriage.

"Hey, I'm glad to hear that," he said with forced cheer. "I'm sure you'll do fine."

He didn't give a damn what I did or how I felt now. He'd moved on.

It was time I did the same.

I placed the final box in the trunk and shut it, striding to the driver's side door. "See you around."

"Yeah." He lifted his hand in a half-hearted wave. I was sure his mind was already back inside with Bridgette.

After engaging the engine, the craft lifted off the ground. I programmed it to take me to my new apartment.

I didn't look back as the vehicle took the main road into the city. Other hovercars flew on either side of me, everyone having some place to go but me.

One problem loomed in my future.

I'd lied. I had no job, no new life waiting for me. Just a ratty apartment and three food packs to create about nine meals in the apartment's tiny synthesizer. If I was lucky, I could stretch the credits in my bank account until I got my next alimony check. I had no other choice, now did I?

"What should I do?" I asked the air around me as the hovercar zipped across town, taking me to the seedier side, the only place where I could afford a rental. Apartment was being generous since it was one room. But it was furnished with a narrow bed, a small kitchen table and stool, plus a dingy sofa, so I couldn't complain.

The teardrop stone I wore on a chain around my neck shifted across my skin. I'd bought it after my loss and worn it all the time since.

I wrapped my fingers around it. Clung to it, actually, the only thing I valued above all else. At least Tyler hadn't suggested I leave it behind. I would've fought him on that one.

Straightening, my gaze focused on a sign mounted above the door of the building coming up on my right.

Intergalactic Employment Agency.

I could swear the stone grew warmer, but things like that just didn't happen.

"Maybe I should find a job in outer space. Leave Earth and never return. What do you think about that?" I stroked the stone, feeling closer to Sara than I had in months.

Halting the ship's program, I engaged the hovercar's landing sequence. The craft dropped onto the pavement, and I got out, waiting while aliens of all sizes and shapes passed me on the walkway.

"This is stupid," I whispered, studying the sign as if it would tell me what to do. Jobs were scarce in the city for those who'd gone from high school straight into marriage.

After pinching my eyes closed, I opened them again. I locked the hovercar and wove around people and up to the front door. I sucked in a breath and released it before opening the door and stepping inside.

"Welcome to the Intergalactic Employment Agency," a robot called out from the back of the bright room. With a rhythmic whir and a bang-bang-bang of its steps, the robot rolled toward me on plexi tracks, extending its metal hand. "How can I help you today?"

"I'm looking for a job," I said, though it must be obvi-ous. Why else come here? "Something off-world?"

"Of course," the robot said, tilting its head to the computerized dash floating nearby. "Are you sure?"

I frowned. "Why wouldn't I be?"

"Lazy days and sleepless nights are no way to proceed through life."

"Excuse me?"

The robot shuddered. Its glowing yellow eyes flashed a few times before solidifying then pointing my way. "I do apologize. My programming has been faulty lately. I'm due for reboot soon. Would you care to come back later once it's finished?"

"Are you saying you won't be able to help me find a job?" Why open the business this dia if the device wasn't functioning correctly?

"I'm fully capable of that. Just . . . please expect occasional glitches."

"Okay." Maybe this was a mistake. I should go to my apartment, unpack my boxes, and then hit the streets, looking for a job near where I lived. Before marrying Tyler, I'd worked in a care facility during the breaks between school sessions. Skills like that never faded. They must have openings.

"Before we proceed," the robot said, "I will need your name and com information."

I lifted my wrist com for scanning.

"I see your employment is limited," the robot said, its voice lacking inflection.

"I'm recently divorced," I said. "I'm starting a new life. My ex didn't want me working while we were married." Or doing much of anything else but cater to him, but I didn't need to share that with everyone I ran into.

"Singing strange melodies of trees," the robot said.

Doubts shot through my mind, but I persisted. I needed a job; this was an employment agency.

"Again, I apologize," the robot said, its gears grinding as it rolled behind the plexi-topped counter, the dash hovering beside it. "I can offer you three positions. First, a Xilan is looking for someone to provide services during his slaking."

"What's a Xilan and what's a slaking?"

The robot leveled me a long look with its glowing white

eyes. "You would perform sexually for a one-week period while the Xilan male is in heat."

"I have nothing against sex workers, but I don't believe that's the right position for me. What else do you have?"

"Flights of fancy result in nine lives."

"Yeah, sure." My laugh burst out, loosening my heavy emotions. If nothing else, this was entertaining. It wasn't a complete waste of time even if the robot couldn't come up with anything for me.

"The second position is for a tour guide."

That might work. "Tour guide for what type of operation?"

"There is a training period before you begin, of course."

"I'm sure." I leaned on the top of the counter, eager. "What kind of tours?"

"Primarily on an asteroid cluster. The owner is seeking someone to take adventurers deep below the surface into the cave systems. You would, of course, have to take the necessary precautions while there."

I straightened, not so eager any longer. "I assume I'll wear equipment?"

"If you did not, you would not only float off the aster-oid, but you would also die within three nanoseconds. Oxygen would be limited to the suit wearer."

"I'm not much of an adventurer." And I enjoyed breathing.

"One cannot be picky when one has no work experience."

Despite the robot's lack of inflection, I sensed it mocked me.

"Anything else?" I asked, my heart sinking. Why had I bothered to come here?

"Erratic words falling from the sky can hit harder than a

fist." The robot shuddered before speaking again. "The last position would require you to travel to a new colony on Merth 4X7."

"Where is Merth 4X7?"

"A planet in the Thrushalon Sector," the robot said.

"Tell me more about this colony and planet." The last thing I wanted to do was accept a job in an icy wasteland—or on an oxygen-deprived asteroid, for that matter.

"Merth 4X7 is located in the Sebula Quadrant. It's an agricultural planet with three colonies, primarily growing hemp. Indigenous populations, none. Settlers, three thousand eighty-nine, most live in the other colonies, not the one with this opening. Water, potable. Air, breathable. Gravity is approximate to this planet. Merth 4X7 is twenty-seven-point-two light years from Earth. You would need to travel in suspension."

Most jobs required that when a person traveled off-world. "Would I need to wear special equipment while I worked there?"

"Of course not," the robot said. "Lizard aliens often kill their prey."

Truly, they needed to reboot this device soon.

"What kind of job would I perform there?" I asked.

"The male hiring someone wants a three yaro commitment."

"Why so long?" Not that I was opposed to taking a long-term position. It wasn't like I had much else on my agenda.

"The position pays quite well." The robot named a salary that, after three yaros, would ensure I could take care of myself for a long time once I returned to Earth. That would give me time to get an education so I could find a job that would support me for the rest of my life.

"What would I do?" I asked, figuring there had to be a trick.

"The male is looking for someone to care for his twin younglings."

My heart clenched at the thought. "Why does he need help?"

The robot leaned over the dash, reading. "I am not at liberty to share those details."

Figured that. It was confidential. "How old are they?"

"Six-yaros-old."

I didn't know what to do. Could I care for someone else's children so soon after losing my own? Stroking my pendant, I sighed.

I could be imagining it, but I swore the teardrop stone hummed.

"I'll take the job," I said.

"Very well. Your com, please."

I lifted my wrist, and the robot scanned the device, programming it and his dash with the necessary information.

"Taste is subjective, don't you think?" the robot asked, its eyes flashing again. "My fuel is electricity."

"I assumed so." I cringed, wondering if this was the biggest mistake of my life. No, that would be marrying Tyler. This would be an . . . adventure. "When can I leave?"

"Now or tomorrow."

"So soon?"

"The male Chullod has sought a caregiver for six lunar cycles."

Nothing was keeping me here. If I left right away, I wouldn't need to watch Bridgette's belly grow bigger, a reminder of what I'd lost.

"If I say now," I said, "could you arrange storage for my

possessions? They're in the rented hovercar parked on the curb outside."

"I believe the position will allow for that," the robot said.

"Then now it is."

A transport pod dropped into a chute behind the robot, landing on the floor with a solid thud. The front panel opened.

I waved to the street. "Let me grab my bag, and I'll be ready to go."

The robot dipped its head forward. "Bird feathers are often slippery."

I paused with my fingers on the front door. "Can you guarantee you won't mess up and send me to the wrong destination?"

The robot huffed. "The pod is programmed to take you to the position on Merth 4X7."

"Alright." Nothing to lose, right? It was an adventure, something I could share with my friends one day—once I had friends, something else Tyler had discouraged.

I hated it here. Everything reminded me of what I'd lost, that I essentially had no future.

Better to trust fate to handle this for me.

With my bag in hand, I stepped inside the pod. The lid sealed, and gas flooded the chamber.

The last thing I saw was the robot peering into the pod. "One last thing."

"What?" My head spun, and the world was losing focus.

"Every westalon is a trite—"

My vision wavered, and I gave into the lull of stasis. Whatever the robot said was lost to me forever.

I woke to the lid of my pod opening.

Sitting up, I peered around a lush, lavender lawn with a

forest beyond, peppered with vegetation from every color in the rainbow.

"A pod, a pod," a young voice shouted.

Two alien children, one with purple skin and silver hair, the other more human-appearing and with dark hair, clung to the side of my travel pod.

One smiled. The other scowled.

The scowling one pointed a laser gun at my head. "Kill her!"

2

FIROH

"Younglings, don't do this," I said for the thousandth time since I'd collected them on the Plushier Space Station.

Patience, I reminded myself. Patience!

I lifted one of my sons off the side of the travel pod, placing him on the clipped lawn.

"First," I said, "we don't point laser guns at others, especially your new nanny." I wrangled the weapon away from my other twin son and hefted him off the pod as well, placing him beside his brother. Though it wasn't loaded, I'd hide the pistol as soon as I returned to the house. "Second, we don't climb on things. If you keep this up, Curron, one of you is going to get hurt."

"I'm not Curron." The son who'd waved the unloaded gun at his new nanny jutted out his lower lip. I marveled again at how much he reminded me of my younger brother while growing up, despite looking so much like his human mother at the same time. "I'm Telsar."

Curron was pure human, from his tan skin to his

straight, dark hair. Telsar had my dark purple skin and silver hair. I recited this in my mind once more.

"Alright, then, Telsar," I said. They'd lived with me for a lunar cycle now. I truly *could* tell them apart. But between settling into a new colony and trying to keep my sons from killing me or themselves, my memory got screwed up now and then. "Please do not climb on the travel pod." Or on the roof, the back of our sofa, or the neighbor's half-wild vescalon.

Easing around them, I approached the space pod that I hoped contained my new employee, someone to fill the teacher/nanny position that had been open for six lunar cycles. I'd placed the ad the minue I learned I'd be taking custody of my sons.

My right leg spasmed, and I sucked in my hiss of pain before it slipped out. Damn physical wounds still haunted me almost as much as the ones on my soul. It wasn't my fault, I told myself again. I'd done everything I could to protect my partner. I hadn't caused it to happen.

Reciting the words in my mind didn't seem to make it better.

I kept my face smooth as I rubbed my thigh. After losing their mom during a hovercraft accident, I didn't want my younglings thinking something would happen to me. I was their only stability in life.

A female peered over the high wall of the travel pod.

"I'm Firoh Androd Brelziox," I said, holding out my hand. She appeared human, from her long golden hair to her tan skin much like the female I'd contracted with to give her a baby—or in her case, twins. Now I was raising said younglings, something that hadn't been part of the contract, though I welcomed the chance to have them in my life. "You must be Molly?"

She stared from me to my younglings to my hand before grabbing my thumb and shaking it.

Heat flared up my arm, but I ignored the feeling. She was human. I was Chullod. While we *might be* sexually and *were* genetically compatible, we were not linked mates. My species sometimes contracted with humans to give them younglings, much like any other alien species, but no Chullod had formed a mating bond with a human.

"Why can't I kill her?" Telsar asked mournfully. He jumped, trying to reach the weapon I'd tucked into the front waistband of my pants. I stuffed it down deeper, noting Molly's pretty blue-eyed gaze following the weapon as it settled beside my cock.

That one glance made my cock kick forward, something else that had never happened to me with a human.

She was an employee, I told myself. She was not here for sex. If she was one of the humans seeking younglings, that would be dealt with clinically at a facility, not while rolling around on a bed.

Thinking about my nanny and my bed in one thought was forbidden.

"We don't kill our nannies," I told Telsar before shooting Molly a smile.

Still not saying anything, she stared from Telsar to Curron to me.

"Did you bring a bag?" I asked, stepping closer to the pod to peer inside. Spying one secured in the upper part of the chamber, I grabbed it.

No, I did not notice how amazing she smelled. And no, my cock did not surge against the fabric of my pants in response to her delicious scent.

"Do you need help climbing out of the pod?" I asked, handing the bag to Telsar.

He stared at it with a sneer I hadn't perfected until I was at least twenty. Truly, my sons were both a joy and a surprise every dia of my life.

When Molly said nothing, I spanned her waist with my hands and lifted her out of the pod, standing her beside it. Damn, she was tiny, the top of her head only coming to my mid-chest. And lush, with curves upon curves. I did enjoy a woman with curves.

She staggered, nose-diving toward me, and I caught her, sweeping her off her feet. My leg barely protested the action.

As I strode toward our home, I tried to hide my limp.

When I realized she felt good in my arms, I chided myself.

It was wrong to enjoy holding this tiny human.

3
MOLLY

I seemed to have lost my voice.

And I was being abducted—maybe—by a dark purple alien with long silver hair secured at his nape. He wore a tunic open at the neck enough to reveal a muscular chest, plus regular old pants like a guy would back on Earth. Except he had a tail, so there must be a hole back there.

He moved confidently, but with a slight hitch to his gait. Was he injured in some way?

"We'll take you inside," the alien said. "I believe you need to rest. Come on, younglings," he called over his shoulder.

I studied his chiseled jawline, his hawkish nose, and the spikes jutting up from his forehead that wavered as he walked like he'd grown clusters of light purple, three-inch antennae.

Despite him holding me against his chest with clawed hands, and his tail that had whipped around to coil around my right upper arm, I wasn't terribly frightened. While he felt muscular enough to rip a board in half, two smaller versions of the male trotted along beside him, peppering him with questions.

"Why do we need a nanny?" the pale-skinned one asked. I suspected the child was half-human. Even if I could make my tongue form words, it would be impolite to ask.

"I hired a nanny because I can't watch you two all dia long," the male carrying me said. He glanced down at me with dark purple eyes that were strangely soothing.

"We don't need a nanny," the purple-skinned, formerly gun-toting boy said with a scowl. "Na-nee, na-nee, na-nee. I'll kill her."

Yeah, that didn't sound good.

"She's going to be your friend," the male said, his voice bubbling with a hidden chuckle. It *was* funny, if gruesome. "We don't kill our friends."

"I have a friend," the boy said. "Curron's my friend." He extended his sneer to his father. "We don't need a na-nee. We don't need you either."

The big guy's lips curled downward before smoothing. "Maybe you do. Maybe you don't. I assume we'll find out."

My heart hurt for him. Why was one of his children rejecting him?

"Why did she come in a pod?" the other child asked, peering back at the unit that was lifting off, returning to Earth. The boy dragged my bag across the purple grass.

"That was how she traveled here," the male said.

Oh, wait. His name was Firoh. The children must be . . . Curron and Telsar. I wasn't sure which was which, however.

"Remember?" Firoh said. "We traveled in a pod from the space station to the colony."

"Send her back," the lavender-skinned child said. "We don't want her here."

Why *was* I here?

Nanny . . . A vague memory of a robot naming jobs slipped into my mind. I'd taken a position as a nanny for an alien on a distant world.

That memory was followed by the image of my ex-husband holding another woman in his arms. Her belly bulging where mine never would again. My divorce was final. Tyler was marrying Bridgette. And they were having a child together.

My hand snapped up to my throat, and I sagged against the alien's brawny chest, grateful to find the teardrop stone still suspended from my neck. I hadn't lost it.

Firoh watched the gesture with a frown. He reached the base of a two-story post with an enormous oval, spaceship-appearing cap mounted on the top.

"Engage the lift, would you, Curron?" Firoh asked, pausing beside the panel. He glanced down at me. "I don't imagine you've seen a Chullod home before."

I shook my head; grateful I could do that at least.

"You know you've arrived at the colony on Merth 4X7?"

I nodded again.

"I'm a Chullod, and while I've settled here with my younglings, I brought some of my home with me." His purple face darkened. Blushing? "I know. Purple grass is a bit much, but I needed to look outside and see something familiar."

Why settle here when he could've done so on his own planet?

"You're probably wondering why I'm here." He frowned. "Curron. I asked you to call the lift."

"I'm Telsar," the boy who looked a lot like Firoh said. They were six yaros old, but big for their age. Big for a human, that is. Telsar was larger than his brother, but they were twins. Curron appeared to take after his human side.

Where was their mom?

"Sorry, *Telsar*," Firoh said. "Please call the lift."

Telsar grunted and placed his palm on the smooth purple surface of the house "stalk".

Truly, I couldn't imagine why Firoh was having such a hard time telling them apart.

A hum rang out, though I didn't see any equipment moving nearby.

"I know what you're thinking," Firoh said with a sigh. "I should be able to tell my own younglings apart, right?"

He couldn't be a mind reader. Maybe my face gave me away.

A dull thud echoed around us, and a panel opened on the side of the steel stalk.

"Come on, younglings. Inside with you." Firoh must've noticed me frowning. "I've only had them with me for a lunar cycle. Things . . . The government took longer to settle this than I'd like. But we're here now, together. I'll explain everything later."

When they weren't around, I assumed.

Inside the stalk, Firoh waited. The panel closed, and a small light lit up overhead, outlining the interior of a narrow box. Humming erupted, and we subtly swayed.

The sound stopped, and the panel opened again to a hall stretching out in front of us. Firoh strode down a corridor with doors on each side. "Stay with me, younglings, please." He lowered his voice, speaking by my ear and only for me. "If I don't keep an eye on them, they get into trouble."

No . . . A laugh bubbled inside me, unable to break free.

They trotted along behind him, though I think they did

so out of curiosity, not because they were eager to do as he asked. I'd already noticed they tried to do as they pleased, though it appeared Telsar was the ringleader and Curron followed.

I'd have my hands full with them, but I welcomed the challenge as a perfect distraction from my wreck of a life.

At the end of the hall, we came to a circular foyer. Planters stood along the outer walls with purple trees shooting halfway up the cathedral ceiling. Firoh turned and started up a staircase, effortlessly carrying me.

"The first level has a kitchen," he said as he reached a landing and started up the next flight of stairs to the second floor. He winced, though his face smoothed quickly. He'd definitely hurt his leg. Would he tell me what happened? "Also, on the first floor, you'll find a library, a dining room, and a living area."

He continued climbing, and I hated that he was carrying me with a wounded leg. But I could barely move, and I didn't seem able to speak. "Second floor holds bedrooms, one for me, another for you, and the final for Telsar and Curron. They insist on sharing."

And I bet there was no talking them out of it.

"Plus my office." He started down a hall with a railing on the right overlooking the stairs and foyer below and two doors on the left.

Despite his subtle limp, he wasn't winded. You had to admire a guy who could carry a woman up a flight of stairs without getting short of breath. My ex wouldn't have lifted me off my feet, let alone carry me more than a step or two.

At the end of the hall, Firoh nudged open a door with his foot. He carried me over to what must be a bed, though it was unlike anything I'd seen before, seemingly made of a million tiny rainbows. Its Firoh-sized, curved, pod-like shape glowed with a soft, otherworldly light as if it were alive. It was flanked by two round tables with surfaces that gleamed like an oil slick on water. Stepping through the door on the left might result in me plunging to my death five stories down on the ground or it could lead to a bathroom—I hoped it was the latter.

Firoh carefully lowered me over the sides of the big bed. Inside the pod, a gentle, gel-like cushion cradled me in comfort and support. It swished back and forth beneath me, reminding me of the time I'd gone swimming in a muco-lake while on an interstellar cruise. I hadn't needed to do anything to stay afloat; the muco-water did it for me.

"Would you like me to set the sensors?" he asked in a deep voice that thrilled through me when it shouldn't. He must've seen me frown because he continued, "The system senses the user's needs and responds accordingly. A simple command might make the bed dim its lights, lower the temperature, or even fill the air with a calming aroma of your choice."

Would the bed take me on a journey to magical places like a silver beach or a dappled forest, allowing me to drift off into restful sleep? I couldn't imagine such a thing, yet here I was, lying on it.

I shrugged.

The younglings clutched the side, peering over it, watching me with curious expressions.

"Can I kill her now?" Telsar asked, though I didn't hear much kick in his voice. From the quick glance he shot his father, I assumed he wanted to get a rise out of Firoh.

Curron frowned at his brother but didn't say anything.

Firoh sighed. "Again, we do not kill our nanny."

Telsar's lower lip jutted out. "She's boring. Shouldn't a

friend be playing with us or doing something other than lying on the bed?"

"She's suffering from stasis lag," Firoh said. "Give her time. I'm sure she'll perk up soon." The sparkle in his lavender eyes told me he was joking about me perking up.

"Besides," he added, "she's all we've got, so we're going to let her rest and, in the morning, I'm sure she'll be fully recovered. You'll see she's *not* boring." His pleading gaze met mine. "I'm sure she planned games for you, and she's going to teach you everything you need to know. You'll learn to read and do math and . . ." He frowned. "Other things."

"I don't like math," Telsar said.

"I do," Curron chimed in.

Telsar tugged on his brother's shirt. "We don't like math, and we don't like to read."

"I like to read too," Curron said, pushing his brother's hand away. "I'm me, Telsar. Not you."

Reading was wonderful. And as for math, there were ways to make it fun.

"We're brothers. We stick together." Telsar shot me a glare. "We don't need anyone else."

I sensed a long story there. I hoped Firoh shared it soon. I'd be a better nanny for the boys if I understood their past.

If only I could assure Firoh that I'd be my usual self soon, that of course I'd step up and do the job he'd hired me for.

"Come on, younglings," Firoh said, his gaze lingering on me. In addition to being unable to speak, I couldn't seem to move more than my head in a subtle nod.

Stasis lag was a complete downer. I hoped it wore off soon.

He took the boys' hands and tugged them out the door,

looking my way again before he pulled the panel shut. Something in his gaze sent sparks shooting through me, but I shrugged it off.

I wasn't attracted to my big, muscular boss. For all I knew, he was married.

I'd do this job and if I didn't want to stay beyond my initial term, I'd hit the employment agency again and travel to a new planet where I'd start over once more.

With that thought in mind, I drifted to sleep.

I woke to a bang that shook the entire building.

4

FIROH

"Younglings," I said, struggling to hold my patience. "We do not plant explosives near the base of our home." Tossing aside the tool I was using to work on the walkway leading to the road passing my house, I stalked toward them.

My wrist com chimed, telling me I had a message, but I ignored it. I'd deal with it later.

"Run," Telsar shouted.

"Eeek," Curron cried, racing around the base of our house stalk, his shorter, more humanlike legs pumping to keep up with his taller brother.

I snagged the back of their shirts before they could get away and hauled them over to the outside table where we sometimes ate our meals. After plunking them down on the top, I sat on the bench, grumbling. With luck, their new nanny would know how to control them. I had things to do. Like continue landscaping our property. Plant a garden. Adopt and train culairs so I wouldn't have to tire my leg by walking into town whenever we needed supplies.

And I had to work in my office. Despite leaving the

interstellar interpol, I couldn't retire. It wasn't about credits; I had more of them than I could spend in three lifetimes. My mind needed to be occupied by more than running herd on two wild younglings.

"Where did you get the material to build the explosive?" I asked. Truly, I had to admire their ingenuity. At six-yaros-old, I never would've been able to do something like this.

Telsar crossed his arms across his chest and sent me a glare worthy of a fellow interpol agent. While I was versed in numerous ways to get information out of a subject, I suspected it would be unwise to deploy any of them on my children.

"Telsar?" I asked, hoping he'd be more cooperative.

"I'm Curron," he said. Tears sprang up in his eyes. "Mommy never forgot my name."

My heart sunk all the way to the middle of the planet. I had to get this straight immediately.

"I'm sorry," I said, stroking his arm. "I'll remember from now on." I held his gaze. "Can you tell me where you got the materials to build the bomb?" It hadn't been much of a bomb; it barely shook the ground. But the last thing I needed was them to build a bigger one.

Curron looked at Telsar, who squirmed, before pointing to the woods.

"I thought I told you not to go into the forest," I said, trying to sound firm and parentlike. Being a dad was harder than I'd ever imagined. "What did you bring out of the forest?"

Telsar's hand came out from where he'd kept it behind his back. He extended it and uncurled his fingers, revealing a small, purple-spotted, green-skinned creature with four legs, a ridged spine, and a purple mane. It stared at me before its tongue flicked out, quickly returning to its mouth.

"What's that?" I asked, partly repulsed and partly intrigued by the creature. It continued to watch me with a lazy look in its eyes.

Telsar shrugged, and Curron mimicked the action.

I waited, again practicing patience. "Younglings?"

"It's our new friend," Telsar finally said.

The creature hopped off his hand and landed on the table, where it skittered across the surface, its tiny claws making scratching sounds on the plexi.

It leapt, and when it hit the ground, a bang rang out.

We all jumped.

"Is it dead?" Curron asked. His eyes welled up again, and he started sobbing, cupping its face. "Our friend's like Mommy. Dead!"

"It's not dead," Telsar said, squirming to the edge of the table and hopping off. He chased the creature all the way to the woods before returning to us, dragging his feet. "Our friend is gone," he said sadly. "It's not dead. It ran away."

I rose and lifted Curron, propping him on my hip. "Please don't go into the woods and please leave creatures like that alone. It must release an explosive substance. You could get hurt, and that would make me very sad."

Curron continued to cry, pressing his face into my shirt.

Telsar stomped back to stand in front of me. "You can't tell us what to do."

"Sure I can. I'm your father, remember? And I told you to call me baji." The Chullod name for the Earth version of "dad".

Telsar's face screwed up. "We don't have a father. Mommy said so."

My heart pinched. He was right; I'd signed off all rights

to them before they were conceived. Still, I wanted what was best for them, and I'd do almost anything to make it happen. I'd be a good father to them if they'd give me a chance.

Despite how unruly I found them; I already loved my younglings dearly.

How could I show them I cared?

"I am your baji, and I'm going to be with you for a long time," I said, though softly. "I promise I won't leave you."

Curron cried harder, and Telsar joined in, dropping to the ground and curling on his side.

I sighed.

That's when the panel to our home opened, and Molly stepped out like a ray of sunshine breaking through heavy clouds on an overcast day. She strolled over to join us, taking in Telsar sobbing on the ground and Curron soaking through my shirt.

"Problems?" she said, though kindly.

I liked her voice that held sympathy threaded through with a bit of humor.

"I'm not sure what to do with them," I said.

"I see that." She grinned. "I guess that's why you hired me."

I was struck by her beauty all over again, something I'd noted but dismissed the dia before. I'd never found humans attractive but now I could see I hadn't met the right one.

Heat flushed up my arms again; something that shouldn't happen with one of her species.

Frowning, I lowered Curron to the ground and lifted my arms, studying them. I turned them this way and that, wondering why I kept getting this feeling.

As I watched, subtle patterns etched into the softer

underside of my arms, and it was all I could do not to gulp and race away from my family.

I'd only heard of this before. It was such a rare phenomenon among my people that most considered it legend.

The legends were true when it came to me.

Only one person could've caused the patterns to erupt.

I'd found my linked mate.

Molly.

5
MOLLY

"Would you boys like me to tell you a story?" I asked, taking in Telsar sobbing on the ground and Curron clinging to Firoh, equally sad.

Firoh put Curron down and snapped his arms up, turning them. He appeared fascinated by them, though I wasn't sure why. He kept tracing a claw along the dark geometric patterns he'd had tattooed on the underside of his forearms. Maybe the tats were new, and he wasn't used to them yet.

When his eyes finally lifted, they blazed into mine.

"You," he said, sounding stunned.

"What about me?"

"*You.*"

Okay. Maybe he was a male of few words. No matter. I talked enough for both of us.

I held out my hand. "I should introduce myself, though you already know who I am. We kind of skipped that part yesterday due to my stasis lag, though you did tell me your name. I'm Molly Evervest."

He stared down at my hand. When I jutted it closer to him, he sucked in a breath and took a step backward.

I blinked up at him. He must not be the touchy-feely type. I could live without hugs from my boss.

"You hired me to be a teacher and nanny to your boys," I said, a touch of nervousness edging into my voice. Maybe he was going to fire me on the spot. After all, I'd slept through my first day on the job. "I want to thank you for taking such good care of me yesterday. You explained what was going on and made sure I was safe, and I'm grateful for that."

He continued to stare at my hand.

I dropped it to my side. It tingled as if I'd laid it on a live wire, but I had no idea why.

"I'm sorry I wasn't with it yesterday. For some reason, stasis took away my voice." I forced a smile. "I believe it's back for good now. I assume you'd like me to get started right away?" I took in the still-sniffing boys.

"You," Firoh said again.

Was he only going to speak in single-word sentences for the next three yaros? No, that wasn't right. Yesterday, he'd spoken more than today.

Flustered by his heavy stare that made my skin tingle along with my palms, I turned away from him, facing the children.

"Curron," I said gently, and the little guy looked up at me with tears running down his cheeks. I stooped down in front of him and, taking the hem of my shirt, wiped his face.

He sniffed and tumbled forward, falling into my arms.

I sat and held him, and while he didn't start crying, he clung to me, pressing his face into my chest.

Telsar sat up and watched us, and I spied resentment in his gaze. Curron might be easily won over, but his brother was going to prove a challenge. After all, he'd talked about killing me yesterday.

I'd show them both that I was here to be a friend, that I wasn't trying to take anyone's place. That there was room in their hearts for me.

I'd yet to see their mother, and I suspected something horrible had happened to her.

Mother.

Heat climbed into my cheeks. Here I was, lusting after Firoh, and he could be married. His wife could be away; that might explain why he needed a nanny and why the boys were upset.

There must be an explanation for her absence, and I was sure he'd share it soon.

6

FIROH

"Hey, Firoh," someone called out before I could delicately share more information about my younglings.

Turning, I found my former-pirate friend, Matis, strolling up my driveway holding hands with his mate, Tatum. He was surprised when I told him I'd decided to bring my boys to Merth 4X7 and settle within the colony, but he was also ecstatic. We'd worked together at the agency after the incident with my partner, and we'd become good friends. He'd also left interstellar interpol after he met Tatum.

"How are you?" Matis asked, dropping Tatum's hand long enough to brace my shoulders in greeting. "We were out for a walk and thought we'd stop by." His gaze fell on Molly.

"Molly?" I said, and she looked up from where she sat with Curron. "This is my old friend, Matis."

"Not too old," Matis chided with a sly grin. "Though my bones do ache at the end of the dia."

"That's because you work too hard," Tatum said with a

grin, poking Matis in the side. "Our home is finished, and now he's working on Mom's."

"And this is Tatum," I added. "Matis's mate."

I loved seeing Molly hold Curron. Would Telsar soften to her too? They needed her in their lives.

What about me?

I shoved aside the thought. The symbols on my arms must've appeared by mistake. She was not my linked mate.

"Wait. Wait. Another Earthling?" Tatum squealed. She raced over to Molly and shook her hand. "Nice to meet you. Are you and Firoh . . ." She shot an eyebrow-lifted gaze my way.

"Molly is my new nanny," I said quickly, noting the color rising in Molly's cheeks. Was she upset that Tatum thought we were a couple?

Molly rose to her feet. She hefted Curron and propped him on her hip, not an easy task since he was about half her size. When I first met an Earthling, back when I was a youngling myself and I'd started training at the academy, I found them a puny race when compared to every alien species. I assumed the ones in training would soon drop out. That they wouldn't be able to take the stiff training.

I was wrong.

Instead, I was impressed by their stamina, diligence, and determination. I'd seen that in Tatum, too, making her the perfect match for my friend.

"Has Firoh been regaling you with tales of when we worked together?" Matis asked.

Molly smiled, shaking her head. "I just got here yesterday, so I haven't heard much of anything about Firoh yet." She shot me a shy smile. Did I see attraction there?

I beat myself up the moment the thought occurred to me.

She was here to work as my nanny, not warm my bed. As for the linked mate stuff, the symbols were a side effect of not having been with someone in a while. I could suppress whatever urges might come from being close to her, control it like I had everything else in my life since what happened with my partner.

Well, other than my younglings. I couldn't seem to control anything about them.

With her here, however, they would soon be under control.

"We did . . . special assignments together," Matis said, playing neutral. He probably didn't know how much he should tell Molly.

"They were spies," Tatum whispered to Molly.

When Matis groaned, she shot him a sly look. "What? It's not top secret any longer. Would you rather I told her you were a space pirate? Which he is," she added to Molly, "sort of. He raids from the wealthy and distributes it to the poor, more or less."

Matis groaned again and rubbed his palms across his face. "We should continue on our walk, love. I'm sure Molly's not interested in hearing boring stuff about my old job."

Molly grinned, looking my way. "A spy, huh? That's cool."

"We can't leave yet," Tatum said. "Me and Molly were just getting to know each other." She sat on the bench and patted the spot beside her. "Sit. Curron's a cutie, but your arms must be feeling like they're going to drop off."

"I don't mind holding him," Molly said, giving both my boys a smile. "I'm going to have so much fun with these guys."

Curron buried his face in her neck, and my heart

pinched. I hated that they'd lost their mother when they were so young. They may not remember her.

I was grateful I was getting the chance to know them, but I'd never replace her. In fact, I wouldn't try.

"Have you and Matis been together long?" Molly asked.

"Long enough to know I love him," Tatum said simply.

My heart squeezed tight again, filled with envy this time. Not because I wanted to be with Matis or Tatum, but . . .

I was lonely. My younglings should be enough to shove aside that feeling, but even with them here, it persisted.

"Matis and I met when he was a pirate slash spy," Tatum said, holding up her hand when Matis sputtered. "I'll keep it simple. See, I stole on board Matis's supposed pirate spaceship to steal something."

"Really?" Molly reeled back from Tatum, her eyes widening with a mix of excitement and horror. "Did you steal it?"

"I would've but I couldn't find it. While sneaking around on his ship, I accidentally poked Matis in the belly with a knife."

Molly gasped. Telsar crept closer, obviously fascinated, and Curron tucked the tip of his tail into his mouth and watched Tatum.

Even I was enthralled by the story, and I'd been there while it happened, though I'd missed her stabbing him. He and I should have a male's night sometime so I could quiz him and get all the details.

"What happened after that?" Molly asked.

"Matis was super pissed off. He made me work as his cabin boy." Tatum chuckled. "As you can see, I'm not a boy, though for some reason, Matis didn't see that right away."

Neither had I. She'd cut her hair short, bound her

breasts, and wore loose, nondescript clothing. Everyone we ran into assumed she was male.

"The object I was supposed to steal for an Ergeepelon alien ended up being a vital component for a big ole baddie weapon, which me and Matis destroyed." Tatum nodded smugly. "Firoh helped too."

I bowed, chuckling. "Thanks for mentioning the tiny role I played in the mission."

Matis snorted.

"You know we'd be dead without you," Tatum said. This was another reason I liked her so much; she had no problem admitting she and Matis had needed help. "We destroyed the device and saved the universe." Her smug grin took us all in.

"Wow," Molly said. She looked up at me, and I realized I'd crept closer, as if drawn to her presence. There was something so arresting in her eyes. Even Telsar, who'd been snarling at her before Matis and Tatum arrived, had crept forward and climbed up onto the bench to sit beside her.

She'd turned Curron to face outward on her lap, and he lounged back against her, his eyelids drooping. Maybe she'd be able to get them to nap. All they did when I laid them down was climb out of bed and get into trouble. Last week, they were quiet, and I assumed they were sleeping. A peek in their room made me bellow. Telsar had opened his window and had climbed out onto the miniscule ledge beneath and was urging Curron to join him.

"Firoh was there," Tatum said. "He can verify this if you don't believe me."

"Oh, I do." Molly grinned. "You're amazing, Tatum. Imagine stabbing your mate, let alone destroying a weapon like that. Huh."

"For a cabin *boy*," I said. "She remained calm and was an asset to our team."

Tatum sent me a dimpled smile. "Thanks, Firoh."

"As for stabbing Matis, you can imagine how that went." Tatum held her hand out to Matis, and he took it and bent forward to kiss her palm. Color shot into Tatum's face, and her eyes smoldered as she looked up at him. "His anger didn't last long."

They'd hooked up fast, but their love still blazed as strong today as it had then. Every time I saw them together, I couldn't help wishing I'd meet someone I could love in the same way.

My gaze was drawn to Molly again. Was she my linked mate? This could change everything. I was already attracted to her. If we touched too much, the urge to mate with her would overwhelm me. I'd have to take care to stay far away from her.

She'd put her arm around Telsar. He leaned away from her, but he was no longer scowling. If anything, he looked pensive.

Didn't he realize loving someone new didn't steal the emotion away from his mother?

Patience and time were what he needed, something I had more than enough to offer. Sure, my patience was tested when they got into trouble, but I was working on it. I'd never parented before.

Telsar slid off the bench and went over to the walkway I was building. He sat in the dirt and picked up a small rock, flying it like it was a hovercar.

Curron had nodded off. He was going to nap after all, though in Molly's arms.

"Matis and I left the agency after the mission was over," I said.

A male couldn't work for interstellar interpol forever, and as my boys' only surviving relative, I wanted to give them a stable home, something impossible while working as a secret agent.

"Matis and I settled here." Tatum said.

"After stopping at my home planet to take care of a few affairs, I came here to join my friends," I said. "There was nothing keeping me on Chullod."

Being there reminded me of the role I'd played in the death of my partner. He was not only a fellow agent but also from my hometown. After the incident, he'd been declared a hero. They'd even erected a statue in his honor.

I was viewed with skepticism and whispers whenever I walked through town.

"You don't have family on your home planet?" Molly asked, shading her face from the sun to look up at me.

"Not any longer. My mother lives on Viacar 3 and my dad's a miner on an asteroid in the Brular Sector. They're not together anymore. I don't have siblings."

"And, um . . ." Her gaze dropped away from mine. "What about your mate?"

"I don't have one," I said softly, glancing Telsar's way. He continued to fly his rock, humming. "Curron and Telsar's mother . . . passed. The Earth government reached out to me after it happened, and I collected my younglings at the space station."

"I'm so sorry," Molly said, her eyes wide with horror.

"Thank you."

Telsar rose and flew his rock as he walked toward us, climbing onto the top of the table and standing.

Tatum's lips twitched. "Firoh was a," she coughed, "fishy donor."

"What's a fishy donor?" Telsar asked.

"Oh, a tiny little . . . fishy," Tatum said with a snicker. "Nothing you need to worry about right now, little one."

"I like fishies," Telsar said, his lower lip jutting out. It trembled; definitely naptime if he'd cooperate.

"Maybe you and I can go fishing sometime, then," Molly said, rubbing his arm. "I noticed a river winding along the back of the property. Whatever we catch, I'll help you clean. We can cook it up for supper."

"Really?" Telsar asked, looking at her with narrowed eyes as if he expected to find out she was teasing by the expression on her face.

She nodded; her face was completely serious. "Really."

7
MOLLY

After Tatum and Matis left, I brought the boys inside and up to their room where I sat on one of the beds and started telling them a story about unicorns and rainbows. I brought Curron in, that is. Telsar reluctantly followed me and only because Firoh told him kindly—but sternly—to do as I asked.

Curron settled in my lap again, looking up at me while sucking on the tip of his tail that was a cute, skinnier version of Firoh's.

As I wove the story from one mishap to another, each time making it clear the unicorn barely escaped the bear's wrath, Telsar hung out by the door, shooting me glares.

Eventually, he stepped into the room holding an odd, stick-like toy resembling a fishing pole. String hung from one end, and at the end of the string was a dangling red ball. It squealed as he flicked it around, and it released a guttural groan when he flung it toward the wall, and it hit. Each time it groaned, Telsar giggled in a demented manner.

"Is that alive?" I asked.

"No, it's a toy," he said in a snooty voice, as if I should know that.

I wasn't sure how to deal with him, but I'd figure it out.

"And then the unicorn magically found itself back inside its wooden stall," I said. "Where she found plenty of feed in her manger and fresh straw on the wooden floor. The bear did not come after her, and only late at night, when the moon hid behind the clouds, did the unicorn bring out the glowing orb the centaur gave her. They remained friends for the rest of their lives." I grinned, savoring the happy ending.

Telsar snorted. "That's a stupid story."

Curron dozed, the tip of his tail still in his mouth.

"Your brother doesn't seem to think so," I said.

Telsar just huffed, smacking his toy against the wall. Each shriek grated down my spine, but I maintained a pleasant expression on my face, determined not to let him think he was getting to me.

"It is time to eat." Firoh stood at the door of the boys' bedroom. Frowning at Telsar, he strode forward and wrenched the fishing pole from Telsar's hands before the ball could hit me in the head. "We do not fling the esalona around inside the house, Telsar. You know this."

Telsar gave me a smug smile. "She said I could do it."

I hadn't, but I could see he was trying to drive a wedge between me and Firoh. Divide and conquer. Funny how boys learned that lesson so soon in life.

Firoh must've noted this too. "I doubt she said you could do it. She probably doesn't know what an esalona is." His gaze rested on me. "It is not a toy, but a tool I use occasionally. I will lock it up in my shop to keep it away from younglings determined to misbehave."

I eased Curron onto the bed and stood, gazing down at

him. Such a sweetie. It made my heart ache to hold him, but it also felt good. Coming here had been the right decision. Given time, me—and this family—would have a chance to heal.

"Should we wake him for dinner?" I asked.

Firoh shook his head. His tail swished back and forth behind him. "They nap so rarely that I hate to disturb him. He can eat later."

I stroked his dark hair that was softer than it looked. Did Telsar's feel the same? My arms shouldn't ache to hold him as well, but I could tell he was mourning his mother as much as Curron. He just had a different way of showing it.

"Let's go eat, huh, buddy?" I said to Telsar as I passed, entering the hall. Despite his surly demeanor, he didn't truly mean me harm. His life had been completely disrupted. He'd lost his mom and moved in with a dad he hadn't known. The only stable part of his life was his twin brother, so I could see why he'd consider the other boy his only friend.

I was going to be here for at least three yaros. I'd show him he could trust me. And who knows? If things worked out, maybe I'd stay on as his nanny and teacher after that. I didn't have anywhere else I needed to be.

Downstairs, we walked into the big kitchen that was unlike anything I'd seen before. A stove—I think it was a stove—took up part of the far wall's countertop. Tall silver bowl-like things resting on blobs that shimmered and sparkled.

"Sit," Firoh said, waving to a fairly normal appearing table. "Since I wasn't sure what you'd like, I've prepared something simple."

I settled on one of the stools, and Telsar sat down oppo-site me.

Firoh brought over the silver bowls and placed one in front of each of us. I peered inside at the bright pink noodles that shimmered and sparkled like the blobs on the stove that could be burners. Green flecks that could be vegetables—or not—peppered the pink noodles.

"Feel welcome to eat," Firoh said, striding over to a tall cabinet. He pulled out mugs and filled them from a spigot mounted on the inside of the cabinet. He brought them over and put them beside our bowls, then settled beside me. "Hungry?" he asked.

I nodded and wondered how I was supposed to eat the noodles.

With my fingers?

Telsar lifted his bowl and tipped it, dumping the contents into his mouth.

"Not like that, son," Firoh said. He lifted an eating implement that looked like a solitary chopstick, and twirled it through the pink noodles, scooping a clump up and shoveling it into his mouth.

Taking my own chopstick, I swirled the tip through the noodles, snagging one and snaking it around the tip until I could lift it out. Since I didn't know what I was eating, though I wasn't picky, I pushed the full bite into my mouth.

Oh.

"Good, huh?" Firoh said, scooping up more.

"It's amazing," I said around the bite. Subtle flavors exploded across my tongue.

"I'm a chef," Firoh said proudly.

Telsar snorted. "Spy."

Firoh's wide eyebrow lifted. "That, too, Telsar, but I'm also a trained chef. I didn't hear you complaining about my merrywots this morning." His smile shifted my way. "My merrywot crepes are awesome. I add just a touch of vane-lest, plus a secret ingredient I'll only share with those who are worthy."

"Me?" Telsar asked, wiggling in his seat with excitement.

Firoh leaned close to his son and whispered.

The boy's eyes widened, and he shook his head. "I won't tell anyone. Promise." He gave me a smug grin. "Not even her."

"It wouldn't be a secret if we shared with everyone, but I bet we could trust Molly not to tell anyone else."

"Maybe," Telsar said, frowning my way. "Not now, though. It's *our* secret."

Firoh rubbed the boy's shoulder. "That it is, son."

I loved seeing them bonding. I'd noticed Telsar was almost as hostile with his father as me, and it hurt to see the sorrow it caused on Firoh's face. He hid it well, but whenever he looked at the boys, his eyes were filled with longing.

"The noodlains are grown locally," Firoh told me. "They're a vegetable, though the loogots," he flicked one of the green lumps, "are a form of protein. The younglings helped me grab them last night. They don't come out during the day."

I lifted a loogot and peered more closely at it, noting the tiny body. A bug? I wasn't sure if I should be horrified or intrigued. While I was sure I'd inadvertently eaten bugs before, they hadn't been served outright to me in a dish.

Telsar watched my face. For a six-yaro-old, he was awfully clever. Having lived on Earth until recently, he must know that some people there would be appalled at the thought of eating insects.

Which was why I scooped up another clump of the noodlains and made sure the bite was covered with loogots before I shoved it into my mouth. I chewed, moaning like it was the best thing I'd ever eaten, because it was.

I might be the teacher here, but Firoh was a fantastic cook.

I'd soon be begging him to teach *me*.

8

FIROH

Something was going on between Telsar and Molly. He watched her, taunted her, and I couldn't decide if he wanted to make her cry or force her to run screaming from the house.

He'd behaved like this with me all the time after I collected them at the space station, and I'd despaired of ever convincing him I cared for him. Slowly, over the past lunar cycle, he'd softened, though not as much as Curron who'd clung to me right from the start. I was the only solid thing in his life, and he worried I'd leave him just like his mother.

Telsar was more like me than he might realize. Until they separated, my parents did their best to raise me. Though kind to me, they could barely stand each other, and that spilled over into everything. I sensed I was almost more than they could handle on top of their resentment for each other. Their mating had been arranged, and they should've ended the relationship sooner.

I'd pushed them more than I should've, wanting something they just couldn't give me. Love, probably. They'd tried, but their hearts just weren't in it.

From the moment I was told by the universal governments that my younglings were orphans, I'd wanted them in my life. I was determined to give them what my parents refused me. Love and a home. A dad, even if they no longer had a mother.

As for Telsar, he was probably pushing Molly away to keep from being hurt when she eventually left.

Should I pull him aside and assure him that, no matter what, I'd be here for him? Or should I let him ride this out? Molly will be here for three yaros, but unless she chose to renew her contract then, she'd leave.

I hoped he'd see that the most value came from the time people spent together. That even if someone left us, we still carried them in our hearts.

Forcing him to do more than be polite to Molly might set him back to where he'd been with me when I spied him standing stoically with his brother, his skinny arm around his sibling who may be a bit smaller than him but was equally capable of protecting himself. As much as a youngling could do something like that. Even then, he'd shielded Curron, and I imagined he'd do that against Molly, trying to keep the other boy from getting close.

I'd watch and see how this went. She'd just arrived, but I sensed she'd call him on any bad behavior. Would he listen to her? He hadn't listened to me, not at first, though he was getting better.

Healing took time, and some wounds never faded. If anyone knew that; it was me.

Their battle of wills was going to be interesting to watch, and I was betting on Molly. My youngling had met his match, and he'd be better for it—once the first skir-mishes were over.

"Eat," I told him, nudging my spellon his way. I scooped up more noodlains and slid them off the spellon, into my mouth, savoring the spicy crunch of the loogots mixed with the subtle spices in the sauce.

He grumbled but picked up his spellon and gathered up a bite, stuffing it into his mouth and chewing with his mouth open, food spilling down his front. He'd done the same thing after he arrived, though I'd caught him eating more politely when he didn't know I was looking. At least he was predictable.

Molly stared at him for a second, blinking slowly, before her low laugh rang out. It tickled down my spine like the finest cloutine.

His face darkened, and fury filled his features, but before he could finish chewing and swallow, Curron walked into the room. He laughed too, rushing around the table to hug me and then Molly.

"You're awake, little one," Molly said, kissing his fore-head. "I bet you're hungry."

He nodded; his eyes gleaming. "I am."

I grabbed his bowl and brought it to the table while he climbed into his seat.

"Oh, yum," he said, digging in quickly. He grinned Telsar's way. "You're messy. Messy, messy. Why, Telsar? Mommy taught us how to eat without wearing it." With care, he twirled noodlains with his spellon and carefully inserted them into his mouth, exaggerating his movements to show off to his brother. "See?" he said around the bite. "*I'm* not messy, just like Mommy wanted."

She'd done an amazing job with our younglings. If only

I'd had the chance to know her, to tell her thanks. I wished she'd had the chance to be a part of their entire lives.

Telsar grumbled, but his dining habits improved considerably. We ate in silence, savoring the meal and each other's company. Or me and Curron enjoyed Molly's company. Telsar continued to make faces and shoot her glares, which she ignored.

The sun set, and we cleaned the dishes together, me jostling Molly on purpose, dripping water on the bare nape of her neck like I was a youngling with his first crush. I wasn't far off with the crush notion.

I liked her from her appearance to her kind way with my sons, to the low, deep way she laughed. I'd never act on it, however. I needed to behave responsibly and messing around with my nanny was not the way to do it.

She giggled and shot me shy glances, and her pretty eyes studied me as if she was trying to figure out my intentions. If she did so, she should tell me, because I couldn't tell where this was going.

But in my heart, I knew where I wanted it to go.

No, I reminded myself. It would be wrong to see her as anything more than my younglings' caregiver.

"What should we do next?" she asked when we'd finished putting the last spellon away in the drawer.

"More stories," Curron cried, scooting over to hug her leg. He looked up at her — he was going to be tall like me— the top of his head reached her breast-level already. "Tell me the unikeen story again. Please?" He shot me a glance, seeking approval. I'd spent the past lunar cycle coaching him to be polite whenever he could.

I gave him a nod and a grin.

"Instead of the unicorn story, how about one about dragons?" she breathed.

"What's a dragon?" Curron asked, his head tilting.

"A big ferocious beast who lives in shadowy caves. It has long claws and breathes fire."

Curron's eyes widened. "Like a culair?"

"What's a culair?" she asked all of us.

"A friend. Kreel and his mate Cora raise culairs," I said. "I've contemplated buying a few pups. They're perfect for hitching to a wagon to take us into town, and when I'm ready to work my fields, they'll pull the equipment to till the soil and help with the harvest. I don't know what a dragon looks like, but from what you've said so far, you're describing something similar to a culair."

"You have alien dragons here?" Instead of sounding frightened by the prospect, her voice came out high-pitched and excited.

Maybe I would talk to Kreel about a few culairs soon. If she wished, Molly could help me raise and train them. I'd held off so far, deciding to dedicate at least a few lunar cycles to bonding with my younglings before adding the training of beasts that would be twice my height once mature.

"Do culairs fly?" she asked, glancing out the window.

Night had fallen, and loogots would be out soon. The luminescent forest glowed already, three stories below. Plants like these only grew in this part of the colony. The planet was quite diverse, and I couldn't wait to explore it farther.

"Culairs don't fly," Curron said, his arm going around Molly. "I want to fly, though."

"So do I, sweetie," she said, giving him a hug. "So do I."

"My baji flies," Telsar said, his chin lifting.

Baji. I'd told them to call me that, but only when they felt comfortable.

My chest ached at the thought that Telsar was warming up to me. I loved my younglings so much. I only wanted the best for them and hoped I could be everything they needed. I could never fill the role of their mother, but I could be a good baji.

Despite his determination to hold himself back, Telsar didn't want to be left out of the conversation. "My baji is a space pilot."

"I thought you were a space *pirate*," Molly said with a laugh.

"That too," I said, barely holding myself back. I wanted to kiss her nose in a teasing way. Her lips . . . "As I said, I'm also a chef. Universe class, I might add, though the dish I prepared for dinner was one of my simpler recipes."

"I think that's wonderful."

My chest puffed. Her opinion of me shouldn't matter.

Perhaps it was time I looked around town for a mate. If I was occupied with someone, I wouldn't be dreaming about all the things I'd like to do with my sons' luscious nanny.

Before I made a fool of myself over her—and before my stiffening cock drew attention—I grabbed the nets we'd left by the door last night.

"Who'd like to go outside and help me catch loogots?" I asked.

9
MOLLY

"How do we catch them?" I asked.

"Loogots, loogots," Curron cried, leaping around. "Me, me, Baji! I'll catch some!"

Even Telsar couldn't resist, though he dragged his excited gaze from us. "I *guess* I can catch some."

"See, that's the magic of this," Firoh said. "Grab your jackets, sons. Let's show Molly how it's done."

"Yay," Curron shouted, rushing toward the door.

Telsar's lips twitched up before he smoothed them with considerable effort. All day, I'd gotten the idea he was testing me, waiting to see how I'd respond not only to his misbehavior but to any small venture I made in his direction.

The poor kid just needed patience. Thankfully, I had yaros to show him I was a friend. He and his brother deserved my whole heart, and I'd gladly give it. I was already half in love with them. Even Telsar, who came across more wounded than he'd probably like me to know, tugged at my heartstrings. His behavior was a defense to protect himself from hurt, and who could blame him for that? I'd done the same thing with my distant parents.

In no time, we stepped out of the lift and outside. The night sky was alive with twinkling stars, and I paused to marvel at all the new constellations I hoped I'd be here long enough to learn.

"Out back," Curron cried, grabbing my hand and dragging me in that direction. He was big for a kid his age, and he'd tower over me before I knew it. I half ran to keep up with him, with Telsar skipping on his other side, completely caught by the moment.

It was hard to maintain a wall, and I hoped he'd soon drop it for good. I just had to show him he could trust me.

Behind the house stalk, I stopped, and my gasp slipped out.

Curron continued toward the dusky purple alien forest beyond the open stretch of lawn.

Luminescent flowers glowed just inside the forest in every color of the rainbow, casting a warm and inviting light over this part of the colony. In the forest nearby, odd insects in glowing blue and green flitted among the plants, and the soft sounds of creatures rang out from deep within the trees, creating a peaceful, calming atmosphere. I should be afraid of what might lurk in the woods, but the grin Firoh shot me told me I had nothing to worry about.

It was like stepping into a dream or a fantasy vid. The warm air carried a light floral scent, and the lush lavender grass felt soft beneath my shoes.

As we got closer to the forest, trees and plants of every shape and size surrounded us, their leaves shimmering with the luminescent light of the flowers.

Awe filled me, and I could only gaze about in wonder, as if time had stopped and I was suspended in the most pristine moment of my life. The trees shifted in the breeze, and the creatures of the night sang with joy in the darkness.

In this alien world, I felt like I could truly connect with nature. I could picture myself sitting outside every night on a patio or even just dropping onto the grass on a blanket. I'd lean back on my palms, close my eyes, and drink it all in.

"Lovely, isn't it?" Firoh said, though he was looking more at me than the plants. Maybe he was used to it by now; the wonder might not awe him like it did me.

"It's stunning," I said softly, afraid my voice would somehow break the beauty. "I've lived in a city all my life. Concrete everything. There are a few trees here and there, and people plant flowers in pots and boxes near their homes, but it's sterile and harsh, not anything like this."

"Are we going to catch some?" Curron asked, his head tilted back. "I'm ready." He held up his trap and a container.

"We're really going to catch bugs?" I asked, not exactly squirming. After all, I'd eaten them for dinner. They'd tasted good. I'd probably eat more of them, plus a lot of other new things, now that I lived on an alien plant.

"We are," Firoh said. He handed me a long metal stick with a plexi hand on the end. "You'll need this, and this."

I juggled the round container with a tiny hole in the top, plus the hand.

"Like this," he said, demonstrating the buttons on the top of the stick that made the hand open and shut. "Catch them and use the artificial hand to place them in the container."

"Why not just use your own hand?"

"They have tiny spikes on their backs that pinch when you touch them. They're harmless, but it's easier to use a mechanical arm."

"Yet we eat them."

"Their spikes soften when cooked."

"Okay," I said. Wouldn't it be easier to grow soybeans and make tofu for protein? Or eggs, though I hadn't yet seen a chicken here. "How do we identify the loogots and where are they?"

"There," Telsar said stiffly from my side. He pointed to a big, luminescent pink flower with a blossom as big as my head. "Like this. I'll show you."

Happy he was speaking politely to me, I followed him into the woods, toward a big cluster of pink flowers. Firoh and Curron entered the woods about twenty feet away, stopping at yet another cluster.

"The flowers are gorgeous," I said.

He nodded. "This is how you do it." Taking his hand on a stick, he plunged the hand end into the middle of the trumpet-like flower. The end disappeared, and he wrangled with the other while poking it around inside the flower. "And this." He pulled out the clenched hand and pressed it palm-down over the container opening. A few loogots dropped inside. "See?"

"I do. Thank you." Maybe this was the start of us getting along better.

I strode over to a flower and put my container on the ground so I could better work the hand. Like Telsar, I plunged it down into the blossom and wiggled it around while pushing the various buttons on the handle.

When I pulled out the flower, a loogot the size of my fist clung to the hand. I yelped and tossed the hand into the shrubbery, reeling backward. I smacked into something and tumbled to the ground, landing hard on my ass.

The loogot crawled out from beneath the bushes and stalked toward me.

My heart racing, I crawled backward, but it kept coming, its fangs gnashing the air.

Telsar snickered and raced away to join his brother and father, leaving me to face the attacking loogot.

10

FIROH

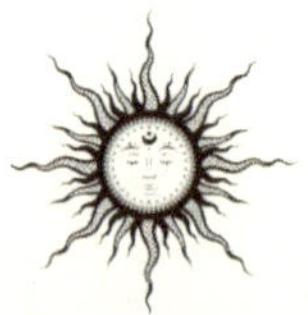

Telsar raced over to join us, biting back a laugh.

"Ya, ya!" Molly was beating something on the ground with her extraction tool. She kept lifting it and bringing it down while releasing one shrill "ya" after another.

"What's going on?" I asked Telsar, but he only shrugged and started carefully plucking loogots off the relaxed petals beneath the main blossom with the mechanical fingers, placing them inside his container.

"Don't get into trouble," I told my younglings, leaving them to collect bugs.

I strode over to where Molly was beating the pulp of what was left of a loogot host. She kept shouting "ya" over and over.

"Hey," I said, holding her arm still and tugging the mechanical hand from her tight grip. "What's going on?"

"I . . . It was coming after me," she said, peering up at me with lingering fear in her eyes. "A big loogot."

"They're not vicious."

"It has long fangs."

"It uses those fangs to hold on to the blossom," I said gently. Would she think I was weird if I held her? Seeing her still shaking convinced me it wouldn't cause much harm to try. I dropped the tools and my container on the ground and tugged her into my arms.

She felt right there, as if building in this colony hadn't been enough to form a real home but holding her was.

She sniffled against my shirt. "Sorry. I kind of freaked out. When it scrambled toward me, I wasn't sure what to do. Then I fell and . . ."

And Telsar ran away from her, chuckling. Would she point that out?

After sucking in a deep breath, she backed away. "Thank you. I feel much better now. I promise I won't scream if more loogot hosts come after me."

"They won't as long as you leave the main blossom alone." Stooping forward, I showed her the loogots resting on the lower petals of the flower. "See? These are the easy ones to collect." I took my mechanical hand and plucked a few off the petal, placing them inside my container. "Like this."

"Ah," she said. Huffing, she shot a glance toward my sons, who'd abandoned loogot collection and were tumbling around on the grass behind our dwelling. "Let me try."

I settled on the ground, watching as she used her mechanical hand to gather some and put them inside her container.

"How many do we collect?" she asked.

"Only a few."

"But a few won't make a meal." She shot me a concerned look. "I'm not a mooch. I'll help pay my way by collecting them every night if need be."

I chuckled. "Gathering loogots is more for fun than to stock the kitchen. I do that at the store in town. My sons enjoy racing around in the woods at night, and I like to make them happy, so we gather a few, and I add them to those I purchase."

She sat beside me, our sides and hips touching, grinning as she took in Curron and Telsar taking turns squatting down so the other could hop over their back. "They're sweet boys," she said softly. "I can tell I'm going to easily fall for them."

What about me?

I wasn't sure where the thought came from, and I nudged it aside. She wasn't here for romance, and I hadn't hired a nanny to warm my bed despite the hints she could be my true mate.

It wasn't possible with a human. The markings on my arms meant nothing.

Unfortunately, it was much too easy to see her lying on my bed, her arms reaching for me.

11

MOLLY

I wasn't going to squeal on Telsar to his father. The boy needed time and patience, not discipline on my behalf.

What he'd done might be mean, but it was pretty much harmless.

He watched me even now, shooting worried looks in our direction. He thought I'd tattle on him to his dad, and that was why I wasn't going to do it.

Firoh leaned back on his palms and stared up at the night sky filtered by the leafy trees overhead. "I love it here. It's so peaceful."

"How does it compare to your home planet?"

"Chullod was once like this, but cities have taken over the surface. Overpopulation threatens the entire ecosystem of my tiny home world."

"It's like that on Earth too, though we do still have vast forests in some areas."

"Once the interstellar government told me their mother died, my only thought was to bring my younglings to the city I grew up in. But I stopped to visit my friends here in this colony, and I couldn't stop thinking about it after I left. Yes, there are dangers here, though mostly from creatures living deep within the forest who rarely venture into the developed areas, but cities can be dangerous as well."

"I think you made the right decision," I said, peering up at the sky. "Do you know the names of the constellations? On Earth, I learned them all. I've dreamed of traveling the stars all my life."

"I don't, but I should learn them. We can ask in town tomorrow if you'd like. There may be someone who knows."

"Let's."

"If not, we can make up our own names. This colony is a new frontier; anything goes."

"You're right." I pointed up. "Like that one. I'll call it culair."

"Why that?" He frowned, and I scooted closer to show him the pattern I pointed to.

"It looks like my idea of a dragon. Since I'm living in this colony now, it makes sense that the dragon in the sky is a culair, don't you think?"

"You're right." He looked down at me, making me realize how close we sat together. "Thank you for coming here." His low, husky voice smoothed through me, making my head spin like I'd drank an entire bottle of wine.

"I needed the job. That was my original reason."

"What about now? I know you haven't been here long, but does this still feel like only a job to you?"

I sensed there was more to his question. "What else could there be here for me?"

He shrugged, but his gaze never left my face. "A new life? A future?"

"I hope I can find that here." I couldn't let myself dream of a future with him. He was my boss, nothing further.

"I hope so too."

Because being so close to him made me long for things I couldn't have, I scooted sideways to put distance between us, pretending I wanted to lean my back against a tree. He kept watching, and that odd, intriguing light remained in his eyes.

"What's the town like here?" I asked. "This part of the colony could be the only section with vegetation. For all I knew, a big city waits just over the hill."

"My neighbor, Cora, said it's like the wild west, though I don't know what that is," he said.

"Ah, she means from Earth's history when people traveled across the land and formed settlements in remote areas."

"Yes, I believe that is what she means." He sat up, and I admired his thighs when I should be staring at the stars I loved so much instead. He had a nice ass too. I'd be silly not to notice something like that. And I liked his long silver hair he left unsecured. It was picked up by the breeze and carried outward before it settled back on his shoulders. Was it silky or coarse?

"I like that you seem to have a simple life here, yet you incorporate the latest technology," I said, studying his dark purple skin that made the whites around his paler purple eyes gleam like the stars above in the dark heavens.

"There's no reason to live without things that make our life comfortable," he said. He scratched his neck, and I took in his claws. His ancestors must've used them and his long tail as defense. And maybe he'd found good use for them when he worked for interstellar interpol.

Hopefully, he wouldn't have to use them here, though he had mentioned creatures. I peered into the woods behind us, and the peaceful setting suddenly felt ominous. But Firoh didn't appear concerned.

He kept watching me, and I sensed the same appreciation I felt for him. Would he act on it?

I was going to be here for years. Things could get awkward if I developed a crush on him. And it hadn't been long since me and my ex split, though I'd stopped mourning ages ago. He'd made his choice, and it wasn't me. I wasn't one to fight for someone who didn't feel *I* was also worth fighting for.

"We should probably go inside," he said, rising. He held out his hand to tug me up, and I took it.

Once I was securely on my feet, he grabbed our mechanical hands and containers and tilted his head toward where the boys lay on the grass.

"They're quiet," I said. "Do you think they're getting into trouble?"

He chuckled. "I hope not, but they're my younglings. Let's go find out."

We strode over and found them asleep.

"If you want to wait here with one of them," he said. "I'll carry one in, then come back for the other."

"I can get one. We can leave the containers and tools here and come back for them after."

"Alright." He lifted Curron and gently gave him to me.

Being leaner and smaller than Telsar, Curron wasn't that heavy, and it was a burden I welcomed. It felt amazing to hold a child even though he wasn't my own. He snuggled against me and murmured something in his sleep. My heart split wide open and gathered him in. Children were so easy to love, and Firoh's younglings tugged at my soul.

Once he was sure I was comfortable holding Curron,

Firoh lifted Telsar, who was bigger than his brother because he took after his father.

Did Firoh have vids of the boys' mother? I was curious about how he ended up with them and what happened to her, but I didn't feel comfortable asking, especially while carrying the boys. You never knew what someone might overhear even while asleep.

We carried them inside without speaking, and into their room with strange beds like mine, though smaller.

"We should take off their shoes and . . ." Firoh said. "Not sure what else."

He really was new to this. I couldn't imagine what it would be like to suddenly take over the care of six-yaro-old twins. Amazing. Heartwarming. And terrifying, I supposed.

"Definitely remove their shoes, pants, and shirts," I whispered. "We can leave off the PJs." I assumed they wore underwear. They came from Earth; they'd be used to it even if the aliens here didn't wear anything like that.

He nodded. "They brought pajamas with them, but they're outgrowing them. I need to speak to someone in town soon about making more." He frowned at Telsar's underpants. "More of these too. I don't . . ." His face darkened, which was kind of cute. For an interstellar agent, he sure was shy about some things.

"Yes, it would be good to have someone make them underwear if they're used to wearing it." I kept my voice practical, nanny-like. "Or they may choose to wear what you do beneath your clothing."

"Oh, er." His gaze dropped to Telsar, and he tugged the blanket up over his son. I did the same with Curron. We walked out into the hall, and he gently closed the door, leaving it open only a crack. "I don't wear anything like that beneath my clothing."

"What *do* you wear?" The words came out before I could hold them back. I slapped my hand over my grin. "Sorry. You don't need to answer that."

His low, much-too-sexy chuckle rang out. "I don't mind answering, Molly," Leaning in close, his voice tickled my ear, "but I'm not sure you want to hear what I might say."

12

FIROH

Why couldn't I stop thinking of Molly as someone I'd love to carry to my bed, spread wide, and pleasure?

"Nanny, nanny, nanny," I said softly as we returned to the first floor and settled in the living area.

"Excuse me?" she said, sounding flustered.

"I offended you. I apologize."

Her grin dropped too quickly. "No offense taken. I . . ."

"You what?"

"I . . ." My gaze fell on a high table along one wall holding tall, fluted glassware with bright blue liquid, plus glasses. "Would you like something to drink? I have something similar to what Earthlings call wine."

"Sure, I'd love something to drink," she said.

As I rose and strode to the table, her gaze followed, heavy and more exciting than it should be.

After pouring some coosair, I brought the glasses over and placed them on the table in front of our two chairs. Sitting, I shifted my tail to the side, so it draped over the arm of the chair, and leaned back.

She lifted and took a tentative sip of the drink. "You're right. It tastes a lot like wine only with notes of a spice I can't identify."

"Coosair is made from crushed berries and trilladeen, a rare spice." It was quite costly, though I didn't tell her that. It would sound too much like bragging. But my family had left me many credits, and I'd added to my wealth during my yaros with interpol, living simply and saving most of my pay. Since I was on assignment a lot, meals and housing were included. My needs were few.

"It's nice."

"I'm glad you like it." She drew my eye all the time. I'd thought once she'd been here a bit, she'd settle into my home and eventually, I'd see her like any other staff I might hire.

Instead, I had a huge urge to get to know her better. To touch her, something very inappropriate.

We sat in silence, but it didn't feel awkward. More like our souls were settling into each other. A wild thought, but I couldn't figure out any other way to describe the connection we were forming.

"You're probably wondering about my younglings and how they came to live with me," I said, placing my drink on the table.

"You don't need to share anything you're not comfortable with."

A neutral statement. Did she care? I wanted her to be curious, eager to know if I'd loved their mother, if I was mourning.

"I'd like to share. Unless you'd rather go up to your room."

"Oh, no. I'm not tired yet. And I am curious." Her lips lifted before smoothing. "I shouldn't be, but loosely, I guess

I could say that knowing what happened will make it easier for me to care for the boys."

I wanted her to be curious for her own sake, but again, it was the wrong thought for me to have about my nanny.

"I was part of a donation program," I said. "*Fishies* as Tatum so kindly pointed out." My smile lifted, and I shook my head. "I can't believe I thought Tatum was a boy. Seeing her now makes it so clear she's female. But she was hidden, afraid. I teased her mercilessly, but she took it like the cabin boy she pretended to be. She's a good friend, and I trust her completely."

"She and Matis seem happy."

"I envy them, though not because I want Tatum, of course. Matis and I go back for many yaros. I'm envious because he's happy where I feel . . ." I frowned, looking for the right words. "I guess I still feel adrift. I'm trying to be a solid base for my younglings, but part of me is still traveling the stars, completing assignments." And mourning the loss of my former partner.

"If you did the job for a long time, I imagine it'll take time before you feel settled. Starting new in a sleepy colony must almost feel shocking."

"You've named the feeling I couldn't find the words to describe. I have to keep reminding myself I don't need to carry a weapon around all the time, that someone isn't trying to kill me."

She swallowed hard, and her eyes widened. "You vaguely talked about what you did, and Tatum mentioned some sort of bad weapon."

"A disintegrator ray." I wouldn't get in trouble mentioning it now; we'd destroyed it.

"Wow, what could it do?"

"Destroy an entire planet, or a species living on that planet."

"I didn't realize what you did was that dangerous."

"I *was* a spy, for many yaros." Better she knew that right now. "I . . ."

"What?"

I rubbed my thigh, unsure I wanted to tell her. I ached to share what had happened, but I didn't know her well. What if she scorned me even more than I did myself?

If we grew closer, well, then I could tell her. She'd understand, wouldn't she? I hated feeling uncertain.

And there I went again, thinking of her in the wrong light. She was an employee, someone to care for my younglings while I completed other tasks. Not someone to bare my soul to.

She wasn't going to warm my bed, and she would probably be happy to leave when the three yaro term was through.

I hated the thought of her leaving already and not just because my younglings would miss her.

I'd miss her too. How had I settled into that feeling so quickly?

"Back to my younglings," I said. "I donated, and an Earthling female was selected. She had twin males. Sadly, she died seven lunar cycles ago. The Earth government couldn't track down any of her surviving family, so they reached out to me. No obligation, of course. When I donated, I signed off all rights to the younglings my . . . sperm would produce." Such an odd term; it made the process feel clinical, but I guess it was. I hadn't had sex with their mother. "I provided for one female only, so my younglings do not have siblings on Earth."

"I'm sorry she died."

"Thank you. I never met her, though I've seen a few vids of her." I sent Molly a soft smile, something I couldn't keep from doing. I wanted to grin at her all the time, like she brought out everything happy inside me. "Curron looks a lot like her," I added. "I hadn't planned on ever meeting them, but I'm very happy to have them in my life."

"Curron takes after his human side while Telsar's pure you."

My smile widened. "He's a wild thing, isn't he? I guess he gets that from me. They're twins, but so different. Curron's more sensitive, which only makes me treasure him more. And I love Telsar's impulsive side. It reminds me of myself when I was younger." I chuckled. "Most of that was beat out of me during training with the agency and while I served in the military."

"Where you were a pilot and a chef. Such an odd combination."

"The cooking side is more a hobby I've worked hard to master."

"A hobby you enjoy."

"Almost as much as flying. There's something about soaring across the universe. You never know where you'll end up, who you'll meet, or what might happen next. Working for the agency fed my eagerness for adventure."

"And now you live here. Will you find it boring?"

"With my younglings around?" I snorted. "Never."

"Even in such a short time, I can see how they'd keep you busy."

"You, that is," I said, laughing again. "They're going to keep *you* busy."

"I welcome it." The smile she raised in answer to mine faded too quickly. She carefully touched the teardrop pendant she wore. "Since you've shared, I will too. A yaro ago, I lost a child. She died before she could take her first breath."

"I'm sorry."

Nodding, she pinched her eyes shut. "I had this pendant made in her memory. It's beautiful, just like she was. She was so tiny. So fragile. Too precious for this world."

"My younglings have only been in my life a short time, but I cannot imagine such a phenomenal loss. How did you get through it?"

Her wry huff shot out. "Not very well. My husband—we're divorced—moved on."

"What do you mean?"

Her sad gaze met mine. "He found someone new. They're having a baby. I guess I'm happy for them. I mean, they're happy, so I should be too, right?" Her eyes glistened with tears I wanted to stroke from her face. I also wanted to hold her and tell her everything would be alright, but how could anything be right after what happened?

"I'm sorry things didn't work out for you two."

"I'm not. We'd drifted apart before I got pregnant, and everyone knows a baby won't fix what's already broken." She drained her drink and stood. "And on that note, I should go to bed. I've bared enough of my past to you for one night."

I wanted to hear everything. "I'll walk with you. Dawn comes early here."

She pressed for a smile. "I bet the boys will be up with the sunrise."

If we were lucky they'd sleep that long.

We walked up the stairs, and I stopped outside her door.

"Thank you for making me feel welcome here," she said,

turning to press her back against the door. "And for listening."

"Anytime, Molly." I kept picturing how crushed she must've felt when she lost her child, only to be abandoned by her mate, the one who should've been there to treasure her and show her they could get through their loss together. He made a horrible mistake, though from what she told me briefly, he wouldn't see that.

A few strands of her pale hair had come out of the arrangement she'd secured high on the back of her head. I tucked it over her ear, marveling at how soft it was.

Her skin appeared just as soft.

She looked up at me as if I could conquer the world, and I wanted to do it for her. I could show her that other males wouldn't leave her to grieve alone.

It was wrong to think this way, but I couldn't seem to help it.

When her lips parted and she whispered my name, I leaned forward and kissed her.

13
MOLLY

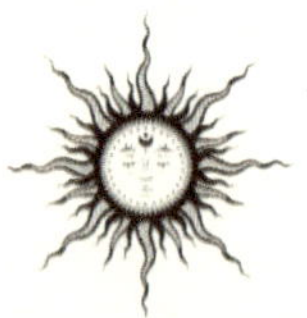

I t felt like everything in my life had led to this moment with Firoh. Like I'd slipped into a warm sea for a swim, and it held me in its loving embrace. This felt right.

I moaned, and he gathered me closer, lifting me up so our faces were even. I clung to his shoulders, parting my lips so I could fully taste him.

Groaning, he pressed me against the wall, and I wrapped my legs around him.

He lifted his head and studied my face. What did he expect to find there? Some women would be chiding him for taking the relationship in a different direction.

I just wanted him to kiss me again.

"I . . ." He shook his head and lowered me to the floor. "I'll see you tomorrow." Pivoting on his heel, he strode down the hall and around to the other side of the building.

What was he going to say? I wanted to know.

Or maybe I didn't. I was quickly developing a crush on my too-hot, forbidden boss.

I admired his ass. He wore pants like a human guy, with a small slit in the back for his tail. His shirt would fit in on the streets back home, too, but underneath, he was pure alien male. A very attractive alien male.

I was crushing on a hot alien daddy. Who would've thought?

I entered my room and went to the bathroom, giggling over the toilet that at first appeared to be a tube projecting up from the floor, but the moment I sat on it, a squishy seat popped up from around the sides, lifting my butt off the metal. Once I stood, the seat flopped back down, lying seamlessly against the tube, and a gurgling sound erupted from beneath the floor.

The sink was similar, another tub projecting up from the floor, only taller. When I place my fingers beneath the narrow tube extending from the wall and ending above the one coming up from the floor, water poured out, falling into a small sink that also appeared, only below.

I did my teeth, put on my PJs, and climbed into bed.

My dreams were filled with happy times with Firoh and his younglings.

I woke feeling rested and went into the bathroom. A clear plexi-covered unit stood in the corner. Naked, I stepped into the cleansing unit. A sanitizer sprayed me from all angles, and I scrubbed my hair and vital bits. Once the emollient had coated my skin, the driers kicked in.

Clean, I dressed and went downstairs, finding Firoh placing dishes inside the sanitizer.

"My younglings have eaten already," he said. "I've left some food in the covered dish for you on the table."

"Thank you."

While he continued working at the counter, whistling between his fangs, I sat and ate. Everything tasted so fresh, unlike the meals I'd eaten back on Earth that were made in a machine from tubes of paste we purchased.

"Do you use a food synthesizer?" I asked, finishing up.

"I prefer to prepare everything we eat," Firoh said, not turning to look my way.

As I came downstairs, I'd debated how I should act after our kiss, deciding to take my cue from him.

Was he going to pretend it didn't happen, dismiss it as nothing, or ask for a repeat? I hoped it was the latter. Silly of me since he was my boss, but I couldn't stop thinking about him, and I felt like there was something between us we needed to explore.

He turned and leaned against the counter, and I sensed he studied me. Maybe he had no idea how to behave either. "I told Telsar and Curron to play in their room until you're ready to begin lessons."

I took a last sip of the drink he'd placed beside the meal, a concoction like fruit juice, though I didn't recognize the flavors. "How would you like me to handle lessons and play, and what will my schedule be?"

When he sat at the table, I felt better. He might not be acting warm and fuzzy with me this morning, but he didn't appear disappointed or angry—a win right there.

"I'd like you to work five dias a week with the boys. Then you'll have two off. As for the schedule, I suggest lessons in the morning when they're more apt to pay attention, then play in the afternoon. If you can get them to nap after that, amazing. I haven't had much luck. Curron will sleep; Telsar . . ."

"Gets into trouble." I said it lightly and with a smile.

"He sure does. After naptime, you could play with them until it's time for the evening meal. I'll take over after that, though you're certainly welcome to join us in whatever we do."

"That sounds like a solid schedule." I liked it. I'd start

with math and science, then expand to other subjects as I was able. "Why don't I get started?" Rising, I took my dishes to the sanitizer and placed them inside, engaging the device.

"Thank you," he said, his gaze searching mine. He stood and leaned against the wall. "I'll be working in my office if you need me."

With that, he left the room. Alright, so we were going to pretend it hadn't happened. I was okay with that, I guess.

Whatever might be forming between us was too new to push for more.

14
MOLLY

I left the kitchen, heading for the boy's room.

I talked them into coming downstairs to the living area and set them up at a big desk on one end with me alternating between pacing in front of them or sitting in a chair, giving them lessons.

"Talked them into coming downstairs" being generous with Telsar. It felt more like coercion. I bribed him, actually, offering to take him to the river this afternoon if he let me do some teaching.

"I don't like math," Telsar said with a twist of his lips.

"Sure you do," I said.

Curron nodded. He'd remained quiet, watching me and Telsar interact and holding himself back as if he was going to take his cue from his brother.

Yesterday, we'd started building a nice relationship; I'd hate to see a setback. I'd come here to be a teacher and nanny, but my hope was for them to see they need me as much as I do them. As for Firoh, I couldn't make up my mind about him. I was attracted to him, and he seemed to feel the same about me, but where could this go?

I didn't come here to find romance.

The boys' dashes hovered in front of them. They'd do their work on the devices and use them for any research and homework, though I wasn't convinced I'd assign the latter. It was all I could do to get them into this room and remain here. Trying to enforce work outside the classroom might be beyond my capabilities. I'd reevaluate in a few weeks when they start enjoying their lessons. If that dia ever came.

Curron tapped the side of his dash and stared out the window to his right. Telsar glared at me.

"Math is important," I said.

Curron nodded, which was encouraging.

"Why?" Telsar asked, just the question I was hoping for.

"I assume you like to buy things at the store," I said.

"I do," Curron chimed in, making me grateful he was here. "I love to go shopping."

A boy after my own heart. I didn't have many credits when I lived on Earth, but when I'd saved them up, I loved strolling through stores, staring in amazement at everything offered. Since we'd established treaties with various species, stores offered supplies from every part of the universe.

"How about you, Telsar?" I asked, keeping my voice cheerful. "Do you like to go shopping?"

"I suppose." He tapped away on his dash, and by the muted tinny sounds, he was playing a game.

When I strolled toward him, he quickly pressed a button and the sounds stopped. "Math can save you credits."

"How?" Curron asked, staring at me raptly. If only the two of them could blend a bit, Curron giving Telsar some of his eagerness to get along.

"Well," I said with enthusiasm, "what if you go shopping and you suspect the clerk is cheating you on your bill?"

"Breelair would never cheat us," Telsar snarled. "*She's* nice."

Unlike you came through in his tone. I had a long uphill road with Telsar, but I wasn't going to give up. If nothing else, I was stubborn. I'd show him I could be a friend, that he could trust me.

"I'm sure she is," I said. "But maybe she's distracted, and she tallies your total incorrectly. If you know math, addition in this case, you can make sure the bill is correct."

"She won't cheat us," he said.

"Well, maybe you'll end up cheating her."

He gasped. "Never."

I couldn't wait to meet the wonderful Breelair. She'd won Telsar's admiration, something I hoped to do.

"What if she adds up the items incorrectly and will lose credits if you can't correct her?" I asked.

He frowned. Clearly, he hadn't thought of something like that. "I suppose it might be good to know *some* math," he finally said. "Not a lot, but some."

"Exactly," I said. "So enter the virtual classroom I set up on your dashes, and let's get to work."

We did math for the next hour with breaks to leap around the room. I called that physical education. We did jumping jacks and rolled on the carpet. Soon, they were both laughing, and while Telsar wasn't ginning at me specifically, at least he was having fun. Softening toward me? That might be stretching things.

After eating the lunch Firoh left in the kitchen for us, we walked across the back lawn to the river.

"It's pretty here, isn't it?" I asked, looking around.

Telsar snorted, otherwise ignoring me.

"Yes," Curron breathed, leaning into my side.

The sun shone on the alien river like liquid fire; its surface glistening with a million flecks of light. A thousand hues swirled in the depths, and strange, multicolored alien fish flitted through the shallower areas close to the shore.

While Curron dropped to the lavender grass beside me, I stood at the top of the bank and let my eyes drift over the water, mesmerized by its beauty.

"There's nothing like fresh air, right?" I said, remembering how smoggy Earth was. I lived in a city and rarely traveled to a place where I could feel anything but pavement beneath my feet.

Telsar skidded down the steep bank, a long stick in hand.

"Careful," I said. "You don't want to fall in."

He grunted and rolled his eyes my way. "I won't." He started poking his stick into the soft mud along the shore, which was better than leaping into the water.

The air pulsed with a rich, exotic scent, a mix of mulching vegetation and flowers I couldn't begin to name. I'd study my dash tonight and learn more about the species growing and living in this colony. Then tomorrow, we could come outside for our science lesson. There had to be a way to reach Telsar, and I was going to find it.

"Can you boys swim?" I asked, taking in the clusters of pale blue grass undulating in the breeze like a sea of velvet, the open pods on the top sending a sweet floral scent into the air. The sky was a limitless canvas of blues and lavenders, streaked with an array of puffy clouds.

The sun was hot on my back, and heat radiated off the glistening water. Sweat trickled down my spine, making me want to scratch it away. I'd love to strip off my clothing and jump into the cool wetness, sink down until it covered my head, then float along the lazy current.

"I can," Curron said with a nod. "I love to swim." Shadows glided across his face, shutting down his humor. "Mommy taught us at the pool."

I put my arm around his shoulders, holding him close, and he leaned into my side.

"Did you bring swimsuits with you?" I asked. I didn't have one, but I could find something to wear if they wanted to splash around. I'd ask Firoh about it tonight.

"I don't know if I have one," Curron said forlornly. He tucked the tip of his tail into his mouth.

"I'll ask your baji about it later," I said. I'd seek him out while the boys napped. "Maybe we can go swimming tomorrow."

"I don't want to swim with you," Telsar said without a hint of meanness. It still lurked in his eyes, however. "And we can't swim *here*." He sneered at the river and area in general.

"Why not?"

"It's not a pool," he said.

"You can swim in any body of water." Unless creatures lurked beneath the surface. I'd ask Firoh about that too.

A forest of alien trees stretched beyond the river, their purple leaves mixed in with orange flowers and blue vines. Every tree branch was alive with a chorus of alien birds, their trills and whistles calling to a wildness within my heart. I felt as if I stood on the edge of another world, a place full of wonders and mysteries I couldn't wait to explore. If only I could capture that feeling and share it with the boys.

Things flitted through the water, but they must be fish.

With little boys, Firoh wouldn't build a house near a dangerous river.

"So, tomorrow we swim?" I asked.

Telsar shrugged, not committing to anything. Curron looked up at me with hope in his eyes. If nothing else, we could splash around on the shore. I didn't see much current, and the water was shallow. I doubted it would come much higher than my chest. Maybe we could find something we could use for floats.

The wind changed, stirring a flurry of alien flowers growing along the opposite side of the river. Tall red spikes shot up through the grass and clustered around the base of the trees. Tiny purple globes dangled from the vines like bunches of grapes. I'd ask Firoh if they were edible. If so, we could make something with them. Science and math didn't always have to be taught outside; a person could learn a lot in the kitchen.

Firoh. He was busy doing his own thing, yet, here I was, seeking him out, if only in my mind.

I could also consult my dash. I didn't need to bother him all the time.

"Who knows how to make rocks dance across the water?" I asked the boys, desperate to find a way to connect. I needed to find creative ways to keep their minds stimulated.

"No one can make rocks dance on the water," Telsar said, as snooty as ever. He lifted a rock and tossed it into the river. It plopped and sunk down beneath the surface. "See? It falls in. It does *not* dance."

Curron grinned up at me. "Can you make a rock dance?" He got to his feet and hopped around. "Show me."

I loved that he believed in me.

"I'll show both of you. Not only that, but I'll teach you how to do it, and you can impress your friends."

Assuming they had friends. They must. Again, I'd ask Firoh about it. I could arrange some play dates. They needed to interact with others every now and then. They'd stagnate here with just me and Firoh, plus his friends dropping by.

"If we're going to make rocks dance, we need to find some flat ones first," I said.

Telsar sighed.

Curron followed me down the bank to the river and helped me find what we needed; his face alight with excitement. Telsar was . . . Telsar. Surly yet curious. Unwilling to let his brother enjoy doing something with me but not wanting to miss out himself. Would he ever warm up to me?

Patience, I told myself. A litany I repeated in my mind.

"Is this enough?" Curron asked, handing me another rock.

"These are special stones," I said with a grin. "Magical, you might say."

Telsar huffed but remained near.

"Come closer to the water, and I'll show you," I said.

The boys followed me downstream to a place where it widened. Curron skipped with eagerness; Telsar slunk along behind us, glaring at his brother's back as if being nice to me and having fun were a betrayal.

They both missed their mom. Was this Telsar's way of holding onto her? I hoped he'd see I wasn't trying to replace her.

Stopping on the shore, I showed them how to hold the rock between their fingers using a throwing motion, and how to aim it at the river.

"You have to throw it lightly," I said. "Not toss it in and watch it plunk into the water." I smiled at Telsar to show I was only teasing, not mocking him for his earlier demonstration. "You want it to skim across the surface of the water."

I snapped my arm out, releasing a stone, and was happy when it cooperated, skipping across the surface three times before sinking into the water.

"Wow," Curron breathed. "It really is magic."

"It's actually science," I said.

Telsar groaned.

"Anything can be turned into a lesson. If you can make learning fun, you'll enjoy it for the rest of your life." Since they were both watching me, I decided to expand my improvised science class. "Ever since I was a kid, which isn't that long ago, Telsar, before you call me old," my laugh rang out, "I used to love skipping rocks across the surface of a lake near where I grew up. My grandfather taught me."

"So what?" he said. He might be acting sullen, but he remained with me and Curron.

"The science behind it is actually pretty interesting. The key to skipping rocks is to get the rock spinning as quickly as possible. This is important because it helps reduce the amount of drag that the rock experiences from the water. When the rock spins quickly, it creates a miniature whirlpool effect around it, which reduces the amount of friction between the rock and the water."

"Wow," Curron said, his eyes wide.

I rubbed his arm. "This allows the rock to skip before it sinks. So when I skipped rocks as a kid, my goal was to get the rock spinning quickly by throwing it at an angle just right. That way, the rock could skim across the water's surface before it eventually sank. And that's your mini science lesson for the day."

The boys tried copying my move, but their rocks sunk with a splash.

"It doesn't work," Telsar said, sounding sadder than he should. His shoulders slumped, and I swore his eyes gleamed with tears.

"It just takes practice," I said, coming up behind him while Curron flung one rock after another at the river beside us. "Can I show you from behind?" I wouldn't put my arms around him unless he said yes; I'd show him another way. But I wanted to give him a little hug even if I was the only one who got something out of it.

"Okay." He shot me a narrowed look over his shoulder but didn't move out of the way when I stood behind him with my chest touching his back, my arm bracing across his. "You're right-handed, correct?"

He nodded.

I cupped my hand around his, showing him again how to throw the stone in slow motion, though we didn't release it. Then I backed away. "Try again," I said encouragingly.

Curron had watched us. He lifted another stone and snapped it out, crowing and leaping around when it skipped across the water.

Telsar huffed and practiced the movement a few times before releasing his rock. His eyes widened as it skipped across three times, leaving a trail of ripples in its wake. "Ah! I did it," he cried out. "I did it!"

Curron grabbed his arms and made him hop around with him, Curron hooting, Telsar showing the first happiness I'd seen outside when he was with his father. As they came close to me, Curron grabbed my hand to add me to the fun.

Telsar's smile fell. I imagined he didn't like doing something with my help, let alone admitting I'd played a role in his accomplishment.

"You made it dance, Telsar," I said softly, reaching out to rub his shoulder. "You made magic."

His face clouded over, and a scowl took over the rest of his smile. His eyes watered, and he shot me a glare.

"I don't like you," he shouted, his hands forming fists at his sides. "I'm never gonna like you!"

Without another word, he bolted toward the house.

15
FIROH

We sat down to dinner.

"I'm not hungry," Telsar said, crossing his arms on his chest and glaring at Molly. "She works here. Why is she eating with us?"

Color rose into Molly's face, and she directed her gaze at her plate of food sitting on the dining room table, saying nothing.

For the first time since I collected my younglings at the space station, I felt my patience with him snap.

"Apologize," I said. "That's a nasty thing to say."

"I won't." His lower lip trembled, and his eyes swam with tears. "I don't like her. Make her go home."

"This is her home," I said. "Apologize."

"No. You can't make me." Telsar stood so abruptly, his chair rocked, nearly toppling over. Before I could tell him to sit down and tell Molly he was sorry in no uncertain terms, he raced from the room, shouting over his shoulder. "You're not Mommy. You'll never be Mommy."

I started to stand to go after him when Molly looked up.

The sadness in her eyes hit me like a Thoksas fist in the guts, knocking all the anger out of me.

"Let me?" she asked, rising. "He and I . . . Let me try to talk with him first? He didn't mean it. He's just confused and upset, and I imagine me being here is only making it worse."

"He needs to be nice. He's old enough to act civilly."

Curron watched us, sighing with sorrow.

"I won't be long." Molly left before I could call her back.

I settled back in my chair, feeling conflicted. I loved Telsar, and I knew he was hurting. But lashing out at Molly wasn't making anything better. She was a wonderful person. If he'd just let her into his life, he'd see that. He'd come to love her like . . .

Whoa.

Like I was already falling for Molly myself.

It was sudden and wild and incredibly freeing to realize this. For the first time, I'd found someone I could care for through the rest of my days. I already suspected she was my linked mate, and it was common to fall fast and deeply with a mate like that. But she'd only been here a few dias.

This shouldn't be possible, yet it was.

"How's the meal?" I asked Curron, lifting my spellon, gesturing it his way. "Have you tried your meat?"

He shook his head. "I feel so sad, Baji. I like Molly. I like you. And I like Telsar. Why can't we all love each other?"

"You're right. Life should be much less complicated, shouldn't it?"

When I held out my arms, he slid off his seat and ran over to me, climbing up into my lap.

"I miss Mommy so much, Baji," he said, sniffling against my chest. "I wish she was here too. Why did she have to die?"

Life could suck sometimes. I'd lost my partner. For so long, I'd blamed myself for his death despite rationally knowing I hadn't caused it.

I was an adult. My younglings were just six-yaros-old. How could I explain in a way he'd understand?

But could anyone ever explain away the loss of a parent?

He looked up at me, his gaze full of questions. I wasn't sure what he'd understand, but I knew this talk was coming. He had his mother's eyes, a soft brown that had tugged at my heart from the moment I met him.

I wrapped my arms around him, and he scooted closer to me, nestling his head against my chest.

"Why did Mommy have to die?" he asked in a whisper. "I don't understand."

Neither did I. They should've had a lifetime with her, just as my partner's family should've had with him.

I swallowed hard, trying to keep my emotions in check.

"Well," I began, unsure of how to explain it, but determined to try. "Sometimes people die because life is too hard. Like, if they're really sick or in a lot of pain. And sometimes it's just because, well, life is too short. You know how you're only six-yaros-old now, and you'll get older and do tons of amazing things?"

He nodded, sniffing.

"Well, sometimes people don't get that chance," I said.

"But why?" he asked, tears shimmering in his eyes. "Why did she die?"

"It was an accident. My people—your people too—believe the fates pull strings from above, turning one person's course to the right and another's to the left. And sometimes, they tug on the strings to bring that person up to stand with them. Maybe they need help watching over everyone else, or maybe they feel the person is too special to remain on the world with us."

"Mommy was so special," he said, hugging me. "You too, Baji. You're not going to die, are you?"

"I'll do everything within my power to keep that from happening."

"Cut the strings. Then the fates can't make it happen."

If only we could do that and keep everyone we loved beside us forever.

"Sometimes," I said, "things just happen that we don't understand. And even if we don't understand why, we have to accept it. We have to keep going and try to be happy, even when we feel sad. That's the only way to honor your Mommy."

He nodded, still trying to process it. "But I miss her." His lips quivered. "I want her to be with me, here or back on Earth."

My heart ached for him, and I tucked him close as if holding him tight enough could not only comfort him but keep anything bad from happening to him.

"I know you do, Curron," I said. "Telsar misses her too. I wish I'd had the chance to meet her."

He snuggled closer to me, and his tears dampened my shirt. I held him, letting him cry and trying to offer what little comfort I could while rubbing his back and murmurs of words that meant everything and nothing.

After a few moments, his sobs slowed. He climbed out of my lap and solemnly walked back to his chair, sitting down and staring at his meal.

"I'm not hungry," he finally said.

"Don't eat if you don't want to," I said. "We can snack later when we feel like it."

"No dinner?" He sounded shocked, and I assumed his

mother had insisted he eat his meals. His voice rose and his eyes widened. "We'll snack and not eat dinner?"

"What do you think, Curron?" I asked, leaning across the table to stroke his shoulder. "Since we're going to eat snacks for dinner, should we eat sweets or make some frescaloop and drizzle it with lots of biergart fat?"

He sucked in a breath. "Oh, can we, Baji?"

"Of course. Maybe not every night, but for this one? Definitely. After that, maybe we could play a game together, either you and me or we can include Telsar and Molly. Whatever you want."

"Everything," he said softly. "I want everything. Is that too much, Baji?"

"Nope." My heart was an aching ball of pain in my chest. If only I could help my younglings through this in the kindest, gentlest way possible.

"Thank you," Curron said, pushing his plate away. His watery gaze met mine. "I love you, Baji."

16

MOLLY

I stood outside the boys' room, listening to Telsar's quiet sobs. Did I have the heart to go inside? Each of his sobs hit me like a knife in the chest, reminding me once more of my own loss.

Could I explain to him that I understood, but that I didn't want to replace his mom?

I had to try. He needed more than just his dad in his life.

I stepped inside, and he looked up from where he lay on his belly on his bed. "Go away. I hate you!"

"Maybe you do and maybe you don't. I suspect you don't know me well enough to come to that conclusion." Entering the room, I shut the door and crossed to the chair beside the bed and sank into it.

"I told you to go away."

"I'm going to sit here and talk. You can listen or you can ignore me." There had to be a way to get through to him, though I'd never force this. Maybe he'd hate me until the dia I left three yaros from now. But hate leaves a bitter taste on your tongue, and life's so much more fun when you can enjoy being with the people around you.

"I never knew what it was like to truly love someone until I was pregnant."

He sniffed and shot my belly a frown before burying his face back in his pillow. His voice came out muffled. "You don't have a baby inside you."

I pressed my hand there, hating again the hollow feeling I lived with every dia. But this wasn't about me. I wanted to help Telsar if I could.

"I don't. I lost the baby before it was born."

He greeted my words with silence, but I sensed he was listening. It wasn't the same as reaching out his hand, but it was a start.

"Love's like a fire, burning bright and consuming everything in its path. When I lost the baby, my little girl, I thought I'd never be able to love someone again. It's funny. You'd think I'd feel the loss of my husband who turned cold after we lost our child. I'm not sure he ever loved me now or that I loved him, but that's a story for another time. Maybe when you're older."

This is when I realized how much Firoh was coming to mean to me already. I came to Telsar's room to speak to him about love and loss, but my words were laying my heart open and exposing the feelings growing there for Telsar's father.

Something else to think of on another day.

"It took me a long time to realize that losing someone doesn't mean the end of love, that a heart can feel love for so many people," I said. Again, thoughts of Firoh clouded my mind. How he whistled between his fangs when he made our meals. How he hugged his boys. And the affection on his face when he looked my way.

Did he care about me the way I was starting to care for him?

"Love's a wonderful thing," I said. "The more you give, the more you get back. A heart's a big, squishy, soft thing with lots of room to expand. You can fill it with love for many people, things you've enjoyed, and even the image of a sunset or the light hitting lavender leaves."

Telsar didn't say anything at first. As the silence grew between us, I remained quiet, letting him absorb what I'd already said. He eventually rolled onto his side to face me. The resentment in his eyes made my lungs ache. It was all I could do to breathe. But the infinite sadness there wiped my own feelings away. He'd lost his mom, and he was mourning. I needed to respect that and not let my own hurt cloud what I was trying to grow between us.

"You lost a baby?" he asked.

I nodded and stroked the teardrop pendant I always wore. "She's gone, and no one will ever replace her. Not even loving a male or a friend or another child."

He nodded, and I suspected in this, we shared a bond. He must be so afraid he'd forget about her or that he'd care for someone else and possibly lose them, even his father. And he must worry he'd love someone in a parent role and one day think maybe he loved them more than his mom.

"Something I've learned since I lost her is that my heart has lots of room to love others. Your brother. You."

"You don't love me." Only sadness came through in his voice.

"I think I could. Is that a bad thing?"

He shrugged.

"I'll answer that from how I feel. No, it's not a bad thing. Shutting yourself off from love to protect the feelings you have for someone else only makes life sadder. You miss so much when you don't open yourself fully. I realize most people think you're a little kid, that you don't really comprehend most of what's happened, but I'd tell them right now that you do. You loved her. She died. And I imagine you wish you'd died with her sometimes."

Tears welled in his eyes, and he nodded. "I miss her so much."

I was crying too. For what he'd lost. For what I'd lost. For what so many others lost.

"Sometimes," I said. "Life sucks."

He jerked in a breath. "That's a bad word."

"Yeah, well, it fits, doesn't it?"

"Yup."

"Emotions are powerful, raw things. They bring a kind of joy that, while it doesn't replace the person you lost, still brings warmth and light to your life. Love goes on forever, whether we want it to or not." I stroked my pendant. "I had this made after my daughter, Sara, died to remember her by. It's not her, of course. Who she is physically is gone. But who she was to me will always be with me. This pendant is a tangible thing I can touch when I'm feeling sad. It makes me feel close to her."

"I wish I had something for my mom."

"In some ways, you do. She's in your brother, and who she was is a part of you. She'll always live on through you and Curron."

"And my Aunt Daphne."

Ah, so he did have other family. That's not what the universal council told Firoh. I should mention this to him.

"She came to our house all the time when we were little," Telsar said. "Why hasn't she visited us here?" He traced his finger along a seam in his blanket. "She's a scientist. She was doing research when Mom died." His face cratered. "She didn't come see us, not even once. We were all alone for so long. Just me and Curron and *no one*. Maybe she died too."

Had she?

"Sometimes things happen," I said. "People make decisions that are good or bad, and they have to live with them."

"It's mean. I hate her."

I didn't know what to say to that, so I said nothing, letting the silence soothe his anger. He had every right to be mad at someone who wasn't there when he needed her.

After a while, I started talking again, hoping I'd be able to reach Telsar's heart.

"I hope you don't mind me telling you about my baby," I said.

He shrugged. Being noncommittal was better than expressing anger.

"Sometimes it helps to talk about it. Other times, you feel better keeping it inside. Kind of like holding a tiny light in your palms and you worry that if you share it, it'll go out. But I want to tell you that sometimes, if you share it, it grows bigger. Like my baby. I've shared her with you, so a tiny bit of her now lives inside your heart. She just got bigger. To me, the worst thing in life is to keep everything about you that's special inside to protect it, only to spend your life that way, die, and then no one remembers you."

This was probably enough for Telsar for one night. I hoped what I'd said would sink in. He was just a little kid, but kids were smarter than most people thought. He'd remember this, and I hoped he'd take something good from our conversation.

I stood. "I'm going back downstairs to get something to eat. If you want to stay here, you should. It's important to grieve. I'm going to go hang out with Curron and your dad because that makes me happy, and life's too short to spend all my moments feeling sad."

When I reached the hall, I paused to listen. I didn't hear any movement inside, but maybe he was thinking about what I said.

Or maybe he was reinforcing his hatred for me.

17
FIROH

Molly joined me and Curron as we were scraping our plates in the kitchen and placing them in the sanitizer for cleaning.

Her face was filled with grief, and she clutched her pendant. She was thinking of her daughter and what she'd lost.

Leaving the dishes, I swiped my hands on my pants and approached her. I tugged her into my arms and held her. She didn't cry; maybe she'd sent all those tears to the grave already. But she shuddered.

I wanted to know what happened upstairs, but that was between her and Telsar.

Finally, she pulled back, giving me a sad smile. "Thank you. I needed a hug."

"I need a hug too," Curron said, barreling into her, his arms going around her middle.

A real, full smile rose on her face as she stooped down and wrapped him up tight. "Hugging's good."

"It is," he said, his voice muffled in her neck.

Telsar peeked into the room, and while he didn't shoot

a look of hatred Molly's way, his face remained shuttered as if he was watching. If I knew my son, he'd continue to do this for quite some time. And then he'd decide if he was going to let down his guard and allow her inside or keep them so high she'd never be able to scale them.

Like me.

I'd lost my partner, and I blamed myself for the accident. In my mind, I knew that's what it was—an accident. My heart kept suggesting there was something I could've done.

Perhaps it was time to forgive myself. I'd done what I could and while some might say it would never be enough, it was in the past. There was no going back and fixing it, even if a fix was possible.

I'd share that with Telsar once he got a little older. If he somehow blamed himself for the loss of his mom, or if he wished he'd done something different, hearing my thoughts might help him feel a little better.

I already did.

Forgiveness wasn't a one-time thing. A person took many steps along that trail, and it stretched deep within the forest. But in the future, they'd step out into a meadow. The sun would warm their face when they looked up, and they'd finally feel peace.

I would welcome that into my life.

"Would anyone like to play a game?" I asked, lifting my voice to make sure Telsar heard and assumed he was included in the invitation.

Curron nodded and shot me a grin. "I want to play."

"Let's go into the living area and set up Astro-Bot. When we get hungry, we can make snacks." I winked at Molly, enjoying the flush rising into her cheeks. If I could, I was going to steal another kiss. We'd have to talk about where this might be going between us. If it was going anywhere.

I wanted to get closer to her. I sensed I needed her as much as my younglings.

Molly could very well be the golden thread that would bind us together.

We went to the living area, and I dragged the game off the top of a closet shelf. I'd forgotten I had it, only recently remembering and realizing my sons might enjoy playing.

Curron hopped around the room in excitement. Telsar hovered in the doorway as I set things up.

"Would you like to play, Telsar?" I asked. If he didn't want to participate, I wouldn't push him.

He shrugged and came over, taking a seat at the table. "I suppose." I wondered what they'd talked about. He kept shooting her odd looks, but he didn't appear as resentful. I sensed he was stepping back a bit to evaluate the situation. That was good enough for me. He was smart; he'd figure this out and things would get better.

A weight seemed to have dropped from Molly's shoulders, and I was happy for her. It was important to take time to process things. Perhaps she'd done so with my youngling. We needed each other. She'd brought light into my life, and Curron felt the same. I hoped Telsar would see how good she was for this family.

"Astro-Bot?" Molly asked, her eyes gleaming.

"Let me explain how to play. I picked up this game on Centurist 4 during a . . . job." Spying on two rival factions, actually, though I couldn't share that. "You have to use your imagination to travel around the board, collecting stars and planets as you go."

"Imagination?" Telsar asked, his face scrunching. "What kind of game makes you *imagine* how to play?" So much for softening. How long could he keep this up? I'd give him more time, but eventually, if he kept acting snide, I'd have to lay down some basic decency rules. Every one of us deserved to be treated with respect. We'd give it to him, but he needed to return it our way.

I pointed to the game pieces. "Each of you take one of the creatures."

"Oh, a vellafoof," Curron said, grabbing it. He tucked it to his cheek, rocking in his chair. "I love vellafoofs."

Molly grinned and rubbed his shoulder. "What should I pick?"

"This." He handed the pink board piece to her. "An aerosap."

She squinted at it. "Looks like a pig's . . . rear end."

Curron snickered. "Ha ha. Pig's behind. Behind!"

"What are you trying to tell me there, Curron?" she said with a snicker.

"Nothing, Molly. Nothing." His shoulders shook with his giggles.

A hint of a smile curled up one corner of Telsar's mouth, and he was still watching Molly. It warmed me to see it even though it disappeared too fast. He'd been sullen with me when I first picked them up at the space station but look how far we'd come since then. He'd soon see Molly was special.

"What do you want to pick?" I asked Telsar, wanting to give him the next choice. I didn't care about game pieces. I only wanted to see my younglings having fun.

"I don't know."

"How about this one? It looks a bit like a dragon," Molly said, lifting a culair and offering it to him.

"No such thing as dragons," he said, though his tone remained neutral. "That's a culair like Kreel and Cora raise."

She squinted at it. "Ah, so that's what the infamous culair looks like." She stretched out her hand toward him. "Do you want to play the game with it? I bet it's a brave, fierce warrior."

"Okay." He took it from her and placed it on his game spot, his gaze carefully avoiding hers.

She shot me a grin but smoothed her lips fast.

My spine relaxed, and I took the fisteen game piece. "The goal is to collect as many stars and planets as possible before reaching the finish." I pointed to the green circle on one end of the board.

"How do we do that?" Curron asked, his head tilting. "I don't see any planets or stars."

"Whenever your turn comes, you'll spin the wheel and move your piece forward. If you land on a star or a planet, you can add one of these to your collection." I held up the small bag, and the stars sparkled through the clear surface. The tiny planets spun within the bag, looking as real as those in the universe around us. "The player who collects the most stars and planets wins." It was a simple game, but that was the point. If it was too complex, they'd either get bored or discouraged.

Even Telsar's face lit up with anticipation.

The game began. Each of my sons took turns spinning the wheel, eagerly awaiting their chance to collect stars and planets. As they moved around the board, they discussed which creatures they were going to encounter in various sections, and who might reach the end first. Telsar loosened up some more, though mostly toward Curron. The two boys laughed and squealed every time one of them collected a star or planet.

They were enjoying themselves, and I could tell that playing this game was bringing them closer together.

Sadly, the game ended. We counted each other's stars and planets, discovering Telsar had won.

"Well done," Molly said, giving him a warm smile. "It was close, but you're the winner."

"I am," he said, his lips curving up fully. "I won!"

That's when I had a feeling that things were going to be alright.

18

MOLLY

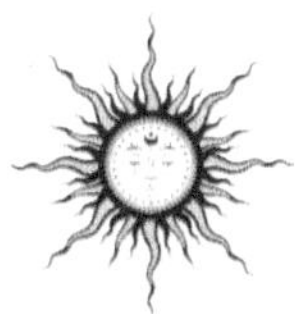

We settled into a routine over the next few days, me working with the boys during the day and finding fun things to do in the afternoon.

Telsar wasn't exactly warming up to me, but he was no longer snapping. Progress, I supposed.

In the evening, after we'd put them to bed, Firoh and I would settle in the living room with a glass of coosair and talk. Our kiss wasn't repeated, and I began to believe I'd imagined the entire thing. He seemed to like me, but I couldn't tell if he saw me as more than his sons' nanny or not.

When I'd been here a week, we followed the same pattern, leaving the boys to rest at the end of the dia and going downstairs to the living room.

"Coosair?" he asked as always, and I nodded. After pouring two glasses, he dropped onto the sofa beside me. "I want to tell you how much I appreciate having you here. I've gotten a lot of work done. In fact, I've finally caught up. It was hard to do my job while supervising my younglings, and as for their education, well, I didn't make any progress in that direction. I tend to jump around from one subject to the next." He smiled down at me. "How do you feel things are going?"

"Well. I try to rotate subjects to keep things interesting. Today, we took a walk in the woods, and I identified some of the more interesting species. Telsar's quite fascinated by small creatures." I liked bugs and frog-like things as much as the next person, but he'd startled me when he thrust a small, six-legged purple creature the size of his palm into my face. Seeing the humor and excitement on his face helped me hold in my yelp.

"How are things going with Telsar?"

I nodded slowly. I'd shared some of what we discussed the other night, and he appreciated me baring my heart to his son. "Better, I believe. I still sense he's watching me, waiting for me to . . . I'm not sure what."

"To leave," Firoh said. He'd placed his arm around the back of the sofa behind me, and his fingers teased the tips of my long hair. "I bet he's worried you'll tell him you wanted to go back to Earth."

"I don't." Never, actually, though I felt it was too soon to say something like that.

"I don't want you to leave, either." His voice deepened. "Thank you."

"For what?" I didn't look up at him; I was afraid of what I might see in his face. Actually, I was afraid I'd only see friendship when I wanted so much more.

"Being here for my younglings when they need you."

"It's my job."

"Does it feel only like a job to you?"

Something in his voice made me look up. Heat smoldered in his eyes. For me, or was he . . . hot for some other reason?

"It's not just a job for me. I love Curron and Telsar. Curron's such a sweetie. He just needs love. And Telsar needs love just as much. We're making progress. He's not hostile any longer."

"I've seen that during meals and when we play games in the evening."

"He just needs time, and that's something I've got plenty of."

"I hope you're in no rush to return to Earth."

Again, something in his voice drew my eye. More heat. We were talking about his boys, not us.

Or were we?

"I can't see myself ever leaving," I said. A neutral statement, but I was sounding him out.

"Not ever?"

"What are you asking me, Firoh?" I held my breath.

"I hope . . ." He pinched his eyes shut before opening them again. "I'd like to think you want to stay here for more than the boys."

"The colony?" I asked, a smile teasing across my lips. A warm, wonderful feeling was growing inside me. "The frog-like things Telsar loves to take home inside his shirt?"

He chuckled. "No he doesn't."

"I've only had to take three of them back outside."

"I'll speak with him about this."

"Don't." I laid my hand on his forearm, and the muscles twitched beneath my touch. Did this mean he wished I wasn't reaching out, or did he want more? "He and I are getting along as well as I can hope for. I don't want to mess with that. We'll talk about the creatures. Maybe we can build a small cage and he can capture one and keep it as a pet."

He turned his arm, tucking it back so our palms connected.

Tingles spread through me from his touch. And when he linked our fingers, my heart jolted.

"What about me, Molly?" He watched me. "Would you miss me if you had to leave?"

"More than anything," I whispered. I didn't dare speak loudly, as if the words could break the spell surrounding us.

"Molly," he breathed. His head dropped, and his mouth hovered over mine.

When I leaned into him, unwilling to escape his lure, he kissed me.

His lips felt amazing moving on mine, like the softest blossom yet with enough pressure to make me gasp. His tongue glided between my lips, and my mind spiraled out of control.

I clung to him, needing something to hold on to.

He eased me down on the sofa and kissed along my jaw, his mouth moving lower, stopping at the top of my shirt. Watching my face, he teased his claws along the bare skin where my shirt had ridden up.

I clutched his shoulders, urging him on as he glided his fingers higher to tease along the edge of my bra. When he slid a claw over one of my nipples, I gasped. It felt better than I'd ever expected.

He eased my shirt up, along with my bra, and he captured one of my nipples, running his tongue across until it became a hard, aching bud.

I groaned as he rolled the other nipple between the rough pads of his fingers, arching my spine up toward his mouth.

His fingers slid down my belly and stopped at the

fastening of my pants. When he looked up, I sensed he sought approval.

I didn't know where he would take this, but I wanted to go with him no matter where he led. I fumbled with the button and then hitched my pants down, kicking them aside.

"You're beautiful," he said. "Perfect."

I wasn't, but I loved that he saw me that way.

"I want to taste you. Would that be alright?" Again, he watched my face, and I appreciated that he respected me enough to ask. Taking could be fun, but what we were building together was new and it could go in any direction.

"Yes," I said. How could I deny him when this was what I wanted more than anything?

He kissed down my belly and spread my thighs, crawling between them.

I felt exposed, vulnerable in the best possible way, and my body surged with anticipation. This wasn't something my ex had liked to do. I'd never truly enjoyed it, because I sensed he only did it because he had to. Yet I'd always thought it could be a lot of fun.

Maybe with Firoh, it would be.

His hands cupped my hips as his head descended between my legs. His tongue moved against me like liquid fire, exploring every inch of skin until he found the spot that made me buck my hips up to meet him. He lingered on my clit, swirling his tongue across it while his finger teased my opening.

Each flick of his tongue shot from my core out to my fingers and toes, and I moaned, my head thrashing on the cushions.

"I love how responsive you are," he said before his head dropped down again.

He sucked my clit into his warm mouth and flicked his tongue across it while his fingers stroked up and down my slit, spreading my wetness.

With a twist of his hand, he pushed his fingers inside me, sending them to the hilt. Like that. Yes, yes.

I didn't know why his claws weren't scraping me, but maybe they retracted?

It didn't matter. My voice grew hoarse from the cries he drew from deep within me.

I groaned and thrust up to meet each drive of his fingers, and my mind spun. My pulse was aflame, a roaring blaze only Firoh could extinguish.

No one had ever taken the time to intimately discover who I was beneath my physical form. No one had cared. Firoh did. He wanted to give me this, a gift I hoped came from his heart. Something that would grow the bond between us.

This wasn't about a boss and a nanny. We were two special beings brought together by tragedy and fate. We'd be foolish not to claim the gift we'd been given.

As Firoh pumped his fingers in and out, stroking my inner walls and pressing down on my G-spot, he flicked his tongue across my clit. It grew hard and throbbed like it never had before.

He hummed against me, the sound shooting through my bones and enhancing my pleasure. Each touch was deliberate yet gentle; loving yet strong. He caressed me as if I mattered, as if he'd only do this for me, coaxing out my gasps from deep within me. A crescendo was roaring toward me, a heavy song he'd created with his mouth and fingers. Something precious and unique to us.

I rode along with him, drawn to a place I'd never flown before.

When I came, it was all at once and with a full body shudder. I cried out, my voice shockingly loud in the room.

He continued to move his hand inside me, his tongue's stroke slowing.

Another orgasm shot through me. I couldn't take it, but I wanted it so much.

"Another?" he asked, grinning up at me quickly before centering his mouth at my core again. "Let's see how many times I can give you pleasure, shall we?"

19
MOLLY

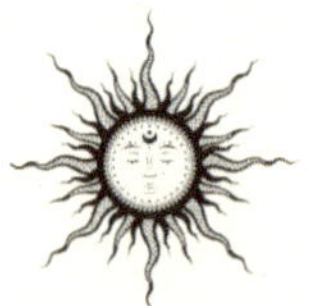

The next morning, my legs were still rubbery from the multiple orgasms Firoh had given me the evening before. Rather than take things further, he'd left me at my bedroom door.

"I'll see you in the morning?" he'd said, stroking my face. He gave me a secret smile, and his eyes were filled with satisfaction despite only me coming on the sofa. A kiss, and he pivoted and strolled to his room. I watched him, waiting until he'd entered, before turning and stumbling into my room and getting ready for bed.

If only he'd joined me for the night. My sigh echoed in my pretty room.

"Get going, sweetheart," I told myself, flinging back the covers and scooting over to the edge of the odd yet comfy bed.

After dressing, I went downstairs and entered the kitchen to find Firoh cooking and the boys reading on their dashes while sitting at the table.

"There you are," he said, teasing alight in his voice. "I

wasn't sure if I was going to have to go upstairs and rouse you."

Such simple words. Why did they make my pulse triple?

"I'm awake." Sorta roused, though I suspected I'd feel more roused if it was just us. His kitchen counter held promise . . .

"Once we've eaten," he called over his shoulder as he sauteed something that smelled incredibly delicious, "I thought we could go into town for supplies." He dished the meal onto a large platter and brought it over to the table, placing it in the center, adding plates and spellons from the cupboards.

His gaze slid down my form, and the smolder in his eyes sparked excitement within me. There was an awareness between us now. We'd been intimate, and it was clear we both wanted more.

"Eat," he said, sitting and serving food for his sons. "Dashes, suspend."

The devices zipped away from the boys and landed on a charging station on the counter.

I took some of the food, and we ate.

"When we go into town," Firoh told Telsar and Curron, "I want you two to behave. If you don't, I won't bring you again."

"Aw," Telsar said around a bite of what tasted to me like scrambled minzir eggs. "Town is fun."

"Then don't touch anything in the store without seeking permission first, and do not run in front of any culairs," Firoh said, adding to me, "many of the settlers have trained them to pull wagons. I mentioned my friend, Kreel, and his mate, Cora, breed them and sell the young."

"You don't have any that I've seen." He'd mentioned

possibly getting some now that I was here, however. "Do you have a barn or pen prepared for them?"

"I'm going to adopt two soon." He grinned at his sons. "What do you think, guys? Is two enough or should we get ten?"

"Ten," Curron said around a bite. "Always more culairs."

Telsar nodded. "I'll help with them, I promise. I'll groom them and clean up their poop."

I hid my grin at his comment. We'd see how much poop he wanted to clean up after his first shoveling. Animal care sounded fun until you realized what back-breaking work it could be.

"I can help, too," I said. "I imagine our two culairs will need names. If your father says it's okay . . ." I looked his way to see if he could tell where I was headed, and he nodded, "You boys could each pick one and work with it yourself, taming it to your touch."

"Yeah," Curron breathed. "I'm gonna call mine Starlight."

"That's an amazing name. What do you think, Telsar?"

"Maybe . . ." His lower lip trembled. "Mommy had a dog named Fred. He died." He pinched his eyes shut before opening them again and released a long breath. "But I'd love to name him that, if I could, Baji."

"I think that would be a great name for a culair," Firoh said, rubbing Telsar's shoulder. "And an honor to Fred."

Telsar shot me a quick smile that warmed me more than sunlight on my skin on a hot day. His gaze left mine quickly, and he focused on his food, but I loved that we were taking baby steps toward being friends.

"We'll walk into town," Firoh told me. "I don't buy

much, just basics to supplement what we gather from the land. I hunt in the woods when we need meat."

"How can I help?" I asked, still unsure how to gauge Firoh. I'd take my cue from him, though I hoped he wouldn't back away like he had after our kiss. He couldn't pretend last night didn't happen.

He watched my every move like a hawk with prey, but rather than his gaze making me nervous, it made my skin tingle. His lavender eyes penetrated me, and I sensed he was curious to hear what I thought about what we'd done last night. Sometimes things looked different in the light of the dia.

"I'll need your help in town to keep these younglings busy," he said. He shot them a stern look, though his lips twitched upward. "Listen to Molly and do as she says."

Curron nodded, staring at me with wide eyes.

Telsar shot me a subtle glare. It appeared I'd have to work harder to win him over, but like with Firoh, I wasn't giving up yet.

After cleaning up the dishes, we grabbed bags and walked down the drive, heading into town.

We passed Kreel and Cora's place, but they weren't at home.

Birds unlike any I'd seen before flitted through the trees. Some had iridescent green feathers, and others were dappled in shades of blue and purple. Most were small. I'd read a little about this planet and while there were dangers here, mostly large creatures living deep within the forest, the majority of the wild species would rather leave us alone than attack.

"What's the town like?" I asked, excited. I'd lived my entire life on Earth, only leaving once for an interstellar cruise my ex and I took before I got pregnant.

"Cute. Small. There's a community center, a main street, a store, a baker, plus a few other shops."

"Thriving, then." I grinned, taking in the bright vegetation. Every color in a rainbow seemed to be represented, as if the forest and scruffy grass between it and the road were made up of rainbows.

"The colony is made up almost exclusively of Ulorns. Hundreds of them settled here. They're stilted at first, but friendly if you ignore how they hold themselves back."

"I'm new here," I said. "I understand."

"They're slender and with deep burnished skin, and they have tiny horns jutting from their black hair." He stroked his smooth silver hair. No horns for Firoh, just spikes jutting up from his forehead that wavered as he walked like he'd grown clusters of light purple, three-inch antennae. "And four arms, though two legs. Fangs. I guess that completes their physical description."

The road snaked down the hill, and I spied the river sparkling in the sunlight to our left.

The boys skipped along with us, behaving for now. Telsar grabbed a stick and kept poking the dirt road and whipping the tall grass on either side, but there was no harm in that.

Firoh paused at the crest of a hill overlooking a cozy village nestled in the valley below, and the boys stopped with us. Buildings in yellow, pink, and baby blue dotted the area. They'd built close to the river, and the picturesque scene made my breath catch.

"It's beautiful," I said.

He grinned. "That's the same thought I had when I stopped to visit Matis and Tatum on my way to my home planet. I left with my younglings, but I couldn't stop thinking about this colony. I knew I had to return and settle here. There's something soothing about it. It makes it easier to put things in my past behind me."

"Like your job?"

"Yeah, that." His gaze slid away from mine. Secrets? He wouldn't be the first. I suspected whatever he wasn't saying related to what was wrong with his leg.

He started down the hill, limping, and I kept pace with him, the boys racing us.

At the base of the hill, he gestured. "This road encircles the main part of the village, and if you need to see the healers, take a left. They're about a quarter of the way around, inside a pink building. Each road leading off this one leads to a home. Everyone builds into the hill. The main road resembles a wheel with narrower tracks like spokes in the wheel. They lead to the center of town. There's a square in the center, though square might be a generous term. No statues or fountains, just a market one day a week where Ulorns sell vegetables, clothing, and even small creatures for pets or meat."

"Cool. Do they hold festivals or any community gatherings?"

"We do." He grinned. "We'll have to go to the next, which is in six dias. My younglings love visiting with the others."

We started walking again, leaving the main road at the first spoke leading toward the central area.

Two-story, brightly colored buildings peppered the outer side of the road, each with vegetable gardens and window boxes overflowing with flowers. Shade trees gave the place a cozy feel, and a few animals lowed behind the buildings.

Children played in the yards, pausing to watch us pass. A few pointed, and one little girl came running out to speak with the boys. Telsar gave her his stick, and I hid my grin. Flirting already, huh?

We reached what must be Main Street since it was in line with single-story buildings. Stepping off the road, we continued down a wooden boardwalk with a rail on our right side.

A shriek rang out ahead of us on the street, and I paused, gaping as what must be a full-grown culair thundered toward us with someone riding on its back. Smoke shot from its nostrils, and when it reached us, it reared back, slashing at the air with its claws. Its red, glowing eyes flared in every direction.

Before it could bolt, Firoh ran in front of the creature. He lifted his arms and made soothing sounds.

The beast's mouth opened wide, revealing sharp teeth, and it snapped its head toward Firoh.

20

FIROH

"Now, enough of that," the older female riding the culair cried. As the beast's front feet hit the ground on either side of me hard enough to make the earth shake, the female slid off the creature and strode over to stand between me and it. As it was a tight fit, her body pressed back against mine.

"Enough, Coo-chee." Her hand snapped out to tap the beast on the snout.

It huffed and dropped to its knees, resting its nose on her shoulder.

Having a healthy respect for culairs, I backed away, keeping my hands lifted and in sight.

"There, there," Moonsten said. "Don't upset everyone." She grinned over her shoulder at me. "Coo-chee needs a bit more training, wouldn't you say?"

I would.

"Whoa," Molly said from where she'd pressed herself against the wall of the general store. "It's amazing."

"It's nothing," Telsar told her with a hint of scorn. "I've seen bigger." Would he ever soften? I might have to speak to him about his attitude, though I wasn't sure that the best way to handle this was. Molly seemed to be giving my youngling the time he needed to soften up to her on his own. Perhaps I should hold back and see how her plan worked.

"Can I touch it?" Curron asked from beside me. I'd missed him joining me on the street.

"You stayed with Molly while I confronted the culair, didn't you?" I asked.

Color spiraled up into his cheeks. "Sorta."

I scowled but rubbed his shoulder. "I understand. Culairs are wonderful, aren't they?"

"Yeah," he breathed. "When can we get ours?"

"Soon." I'd speak to Kreel about it next week. His mating pair should have new pups soon.

I strode over to stand with Moonsten. "When did you get a pup?" I'd missed the news.

"Oh, a bit ago," she said. "Everyone's talking about them. I felt I should join in on the fun."

How had I missed that she'd adopted one? As our most senior elder, I shuddered at the thought of her working with a beast this size, but culairs were basically gentle creatures. If she'd raised it from a pup, it must love her.

As if to punctuate my thought, it nudged her with its snout, and she laughed, shoved a step backward.

"I see a new female has arrived in town," she said.

"Molly," I called out. "Come meet Moonsten."

She joined us, though she remained behind me, shooting the culair wide-eyed looks. "It's incredible."

"Molly?" I said. "This is Moonsten, one of the town's elders. While Kreel is the town manager, the elders make many of the decisions in consultation with him. They write and enforce laws, and if you've got a problem with anyone in town, seek one of them and they'll be glad to help you." I nodded to our elder. "Molly recently arrived to help me care for my younglings."

"Who are getting into trouble," Moonsten said, waving to where Telsar was walking precariously along the side of a watering trough, his hands outstretched, a big grin on his face.

I shook my head and strode over to lift him off. "Son. Please."

Curron stood nearby on the walkway. "I told him not to do it."

"I'm sure you did." I carried Telsar over to the ladies, depositing him on the ground but keeping a tight grip on the back of his shirt. Curron came over to lean against Molly, and she put her arm around him.

"I can see why you hired someone," Moonsten said, her eyes sparkling. "Well, I need to get to the office for a meeting." With a nod, she leapt up onto the culair's back and guided the creature around us. It walked placidly toward the building where she met with the other elders.

"The store is there," I said, pointing. "Come with me, Telsar." I shot him a lifted brow warning to behave. "If you don't get into any more trouble, I'll get you a treat in the store."

He grunted but nodded, which was enough for me.

Curron took Molly's hand and skipped along with us up onto the boardwalk and inside the store, where we approached the counter.

"Look around, younglings," I said. "If you see something you cannot live without, show me. And behave."

"Don't touch anything that might break," Molly said. "Don't climb on anything, and do not leave the store without permission."

Curron nodded, his wide-eyed gaze focused on her face.

Telsar grunted again and started weaving up and down the aisles.

I approached the counter with Molly.

"Welcome," the female standing behind the counter said with a soft dip of her head. Her blue eyes sparkled as they passed from me to Molly and my younglings. "How can I help you, Firoh?"

"Molly?" I said. "This is Breelair, one of the sweetest people in town. Breelair, this is Molly."

"Ah, wonderful," Breelair said, clapping her hands. Grinning, she rested them on her very pregnant belly. She and her mate, Aircorn, were expecting their first youngling at any time. "Nice to meet you, Molly."

"Nice to meet you," Molly said. She peered around with the same wonder as Curron, taking in all the items for sale. "Such a great store. I guess I thought the options would be limited, but you've got everything."

"Yes," Breelair said. "We had made arrangements for irregular supply runs to keep us stocked, but Matis and his mate, Tatum, now handle all of that for us. They ensure we have everything we need." She rounded the counter and approached a rack of clothing, removing an item and holding it up. "Look! Two sleeves, not four." Her chuckle rang out. "As you can see, Ulorns have four arms, but with humans and other species settling here, we try to accommodate everyone. There isn't anything you need that we can't find a way to provide."

"This is great," Molly said, strolling around the items for sale. "I brought a bag with a few things, but I'm sure I'll need something new eventually."

"Pick out some things now, if you'd like," I said.

"Oh, um." Color rose in her face. "I neglected to load

credits on my com before I left Earth." She tapped her wrist device. "I'll see if I can get some loaded before we come to town next."

"I'm happy to provide things for you," I said. "I appreciate you coming here so quickly." I nodded to Breelair. "Would you help Molly pick out five or six outfits? And personal items, if she has need."

"That's sweet of you," Molly said, directing her gaze to the wooden floorboards. "I'll pay you back."

"We can discuss that later."

"What do you think of this?" Breelair asked, holding up a dress.

Molly passed me, approaching the other female. "So pretty." She shot a grin at me over her shoulder. "Maybe I'll need something to wear on a date."

21
MOLLY

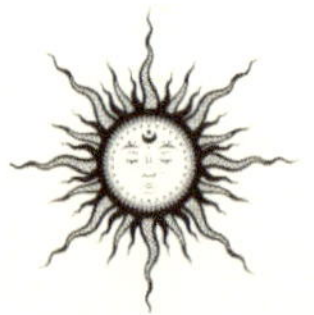

Of course, when I mentioned dating, I could only think of Firoh.

"Dating?" he asked with a lifted brow.

I couldn't read his expression, but his eyes remained neutral.

"I suppose," I said. "If I met someone I wanted to date." I turned to Breelair. "Are there places to go for something like that?"

"My mate, Aircorn, had expanded his bakery," she said. "Cora urged him to do so. Now people can sit and enjoy a coo-kees, a beverage, or even a slice of bread my mate bakes himself."

"That sounds wonderful," I said. I hadn't expected to find restaurants here, but maybe Firoh and I could come into town sometime and have a snack and a drink at Aircorn's place.

"Oh," Breelair said as I strolled around the racks, pulling out a few items and laying them over my arm. "I nearly forgot." She bustled up to the counter and stooped down behind it. "Someone has been trying to reach you, Firoh, and they sent a missive to the store on the chance you would stop by, and I could deliver it." She handed him an old-fashioned holodisk.

"Thank you." He placed it in his pocket. "I'll look at it later."

"These might need to be altered unless you have them in different sizes," I said, laying three outfits on the counter.

"I can alter them quickly," Breelair said. "If you'd like to wait?"

"Why don't we go to the bakery for a cookie?" Firoh said.

The boys squealed and jumped up and down. Cookies appeared to be a universal thing. I hadn't thought anyone would know what they were this far from Earth. Maybe it was a different sort of sweet and they called it a cookie. It might end up being a bug-peppered salty snack, and I'd be disappointed.

"Would you like that?" Firoh asked, his sparkling eyes turning my way.

I nodded. There were so many things I'd like when it came to Firoh. Would it be horrible to fall for my boss? Probably. He would find a mate here and tell me my services were no longer needed.

"Give me thirty minues or so," Breelair said. "And I will be finished." Striding around the counter, she stopped at the big window looking out at the street and pointed to our left. "My Aircorn's bakery is that way. Follow the delicious smell." Her laugh burst out.

Peering around, I was surprised to find the boys standing near a shelf full of toys. They weren't climbing on it or pulling everything off to throw them on the floor, something I suspected Telsar might do if given the chance.

"Have you found something you'd like?" I called out to them.

Curron nodded and tugged a dellarine off the shelf, bringing it over to place on the counter with the rest of our things.

Telsar followed with a second dellarine.

"You two will have fun digging in the dirt with these," I said. "Great choice."

Firoh added more things to our order, various food items I'd never seen before but wanted to try.

"Will that be all?" Breelair asked after loading everything into the packs we'd carried from the house.

"Yes, thank you." Firoh paid with a click of his com, and we left the store, taking a left.

Breelair was right, the lovely, sweet smell of baked goods drew me toward the bakery and by the time we entered, I was salivating.

Aircorn had set up tables outside the bakery, and a few Ulorns sat eating, enjoying the sunshine and each other's company. We passed them, Firoh dipping his head and them murmuring greetings and entered the small shop.

A few tables with delicate chairs had been placed inside. We approached a clear plexi display case. Behind it, a wall of shelves held various kinds of bread. An Ulorn who must be Aircorn bustled through the door between the shelves.

"Well," he said in a boisterous voice. "Welcome!"

"Breelair sent us," I said. "I heard you have cookies?"

"That and so many other treats." His grin revealed his fangs. He waved with one of his four arms at the display case. "We have many Earth treats to offer. Cora has kindly shared many recipes, and I will note that I have perfected them." He leaned over the counter, lowering his voice.

"Please tell her that, would you? That my treats are much better than hers." From the sly but happy gleam in his eyes, I sensed there was a healthy competition going on between them.

"I'll have to taste before I can decide," I said.

"You are correct." He took a cookie from the case and broke it into pieces, handing each of us one. "I have been practicing with the cocoa beans I obtained from Earth, and I do believe my choo-co-lat is better than hers."

He watched as we nibbled on the cookie.

"Amazing," I said around the bite. "Truly amazing. I'll tell Cora." Actually, I'd ask Cora for a sample of her cookies, or two or three, and decide after that, but there was no reason to tell Aircorn that.

"Maybe we should hold a bake-off?" Firoh asked. "I'm an excellent chef, and my pastries were featured in an interstellar blitz."

Aircorn grunted. "I accept your challenge. I am sure Cora will join in." His voice lifted in excitement. "We'll hold it during our next village meet up at the community center. Do you have your ingredients?" he asked Firoh.

"I do." Firoh extended his hand over the counter, and they bumped fists. "May the best baker win."

22

FIROH

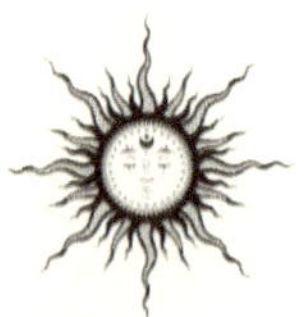

"Breelair is altering some clothing for me," Molly told Aircorn.

"My lovely mate." His face darkened. "We will soon welcome the first of many younglings." His envious gaze took in my boys chattering about the treats on display. "Many. Tell me, Firoh, have you considered having more younglings yourself?" His attention swept to Molly, who studiously studied the cookies inside the counter.

"Perhaps someday," I said. All I could picture was Molly holding our young, a thought I needed to push away.

"What about you, Molly?" Aircorn asked.

"Oh," she said sadly, running her pendant across the chain around her neck. "I love younglings, but I can't have them. Something happened . . ." Shadows lurked in her gaze, and tears glistened. "I love younglings, but I won't be having any myself."

I hadn't realized she couldn't have more.

"What would you like?" I asked my boys, jumping in with a distraction.

They hopped around, pointing at the items on display inside a wide, clear-plexi case.

"Can I have that and that and that?" Curron asked, poking his finger at one thing after another. "I want it all!"

"Pick two," I said. "We'll eat one now while we wait for Breelair to alter Molly's clothing, then bring the others home to have after dinner."

"Okay," Curron said, a frown knitting his forehead. "One of those and one of those." He watched eagerly as Aircorn used tongs to place his choice on a pretty plate that he handed over to Curron.

"Anything to drink?" Aircorn asked, bustling behind the counter, placing our treats on other plates.

"Water?" I asked, and he nodded and filled cups at a sink along one wall, handing them over to us.

We took our cookies outside and sat at one of the tables.

The holodisk shifted inside my pocket, and I was reminded of the com message I got the other day that I completely forgot about. Were they connected? Probably not. I got lots of messages related to my business.

Molly shot me a sweet smile. "I appreciate everything you're doing for me today." The younglings ate their cookies fast, then played with their water, dipping their claws in and flicking droplets at each other. Without interrupting, Molly lifted Curron off his seat and placed him on another, far enough away from Telsar that he couldn't reach with water. "I feel grateful I found this job."

And I was grateful she'd come into my life. How could I convince her to stay forever?

"Stay close, younglings," Molly called out as we strode through town, heading home after collecting the rest of our things.

Telsar bolted along the walkway. Curron hung with her, holding her hand.

He was bonding with her already, and I could see why he did. I ached to bond with her myself, though in a different way. Telsar would take time, but I was confident he'd soon feel the same. Molly was such a sweet person, loving and gentle with them, kind too. She was perfect for our family.

For me, as well.

We left town, striding up the hill. My thoughts whirled. I wanted her, but like with Telsar, I didn't want to rush this. My forearms tingled all the time, and the symbols on the undersides etched deeper.

She was my true mate, and I rejoiced that I'd found her.

"You're quiet," she said, shooting me a look I couldn't define.

"Just thinking."

She nodded. "I get introspective sometimes too." She fingered her teardrop pendant, reminding me of her loss.

Hearing she couldn't have more young shocked me, but it didn't change my feelings a bit. I still wanted her in my life. *Her.* Not what she could bring me other than her heart.

We arrived home and went inside. I paused in the living area, pulling out the holodisk.

"I was going to—" Molly said from the open doorway as the image appeared in front of me.

It was a human male about my parent's age. I didn't recognize him.

"As a representative of the Interstellar Communication

Network, I've been trying to reach you. We sent a message via your com, but you did not reply."

"Let me come back in a bit," Molly said.

I held up my hand, indicating she could stay. This must be nothing. Perhaps something related to the agency.

"She'll arrive at the colony soon," the male said. "Please have the younglings ready."

The message winked out.

"What's that about?" Molly asked, joining me in the middle of the room.

"Where are the boys?" I asked, my gut clenching tight. This wasn't about the agency.

The Interstellar Communication Network was the first to reach out to me after the boy's mother died.

"They're in their room. Playing nicely, I hope," she said with a soft laugh. "I won't leave them for long." Her smile faded. "I didn't understand the communication, did you?"

"He mentioned a prior message. Something came through on my com the other day, but I forgot to view it. I didn't recognize the sender and assumed it was spam." Lifting my wrist com, I scrolled through until I found it.

When it popped up, I read it aloud. "It's from the Interstellar Communication Network. Dear Firoh, Brenda Blaisdell's sister has come forward to claim the younglings Telsar and Curron. When she didn't initially respond to our messages, we assumed she was not interested in assuming their care. Our mistake, but we will rectify it immediately. Her shuttle will arrive . . ." A date and time were indicated in the message.

My belly dropped to the middle of the planet.

"What does this mean?" Molly asked.

"Brenda's sister will be here tomorrow to collect my sons."

23
MOLLY

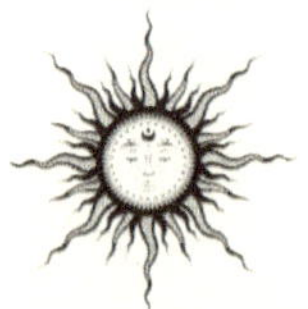

"But you're their father," I said, shock pouring through me. I hurried to the sliding doors leading to the foyer and closed them. The boys didn't need to hear this.

"I signed away all parental rights," he said bleakly, still staring at his com. "They're mine, but they must legally belong to Daphne's family should they choose to claim that right."

"The government must've signed them over to you." I shook my head. "I'm not sure that's the right term for it, but you must have legal custody now."

"I do." He shoved out a sigh. "When I collected them on the space station, I endorsed all the necessary paperwork. They're my younglings, and I'm not going to relinquish them to someone else."

"Can you send her away?"

He shrugged. "I'll tell her she has no claim, though it appears the interstellar government believes she does."

"Telsar mentioned his aunt the other day, that he was upset that she hadn't come home after their mother died. I'm sorry. I forgot to tell you."

"It's alright. We've been busy."

"Her name's Daphne." Resolve filled me. "When she gets here, we'll send her away."

"Molly." He stroked my face. "I can't face this alone. Knowing you're here to stand beside me is going to make a huge difference no matter what happens."

If Daphne took the boys, I'd have no job, though that was very low on my priority list.

"I'm sorry this is happening. You've just started to bond with them. I can tell you already love them, and they adore you."

"Curron? Yes. I'm less sure about Telsar," he said with a soft laugh. "It's a work in progress."

"He cares. He's just wounded and doesn't know how to work through his feelings. With time, he'll come around." If Firoh was given the time he needed. "What can we do?" I asked again.

"I'm going to speak with Moonsten. She and the other elders have jurisdiction over the colony. Yes, the interstellar government makes final decisions, but they rarely intervene with local councils."

"There's hope, then, that Moonsten and the others will tell Daphne's sister she can't take your sons?"

"I hope so." Growling, he stared at the wall. "I do not know what to do other than appeal to the elders."

Stepping forward, I wrapped my arms around him. "I'm here with you no matter what." It was too soon to speak of emotions. I liked him a lot. I wanted more.

His arms went around me. "This means everything to me."

We'd retain custody of his sons.

Any way we could.

24

FIROH

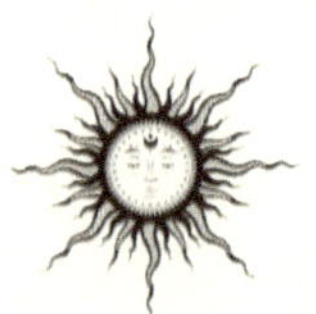

I cooked my younglings' favorite meal for dinner.

"This is good, Baji," Telsar said. His voice was so earnest, and the gaze he sent my way so happy, it broke my heart.

"It really is," Curron said, shoving in another bite. He mumbled around it. "Make more. Every night!"

We laughed, but I could tell Molly's heart wasn't in it any more than mine.

"Who'd like to play spindelar?" I asked after we'd cleaned up the dishes, something we all did together like a real family.

"Me, me," Curron cried, jumping around.

"What's spindelar?" Molly asked, her pretty eyes gleaming.

"A game where the players are real," Telsar breathed, his face bright with excitement. We were slowly growing closer, and he'd be taken from me.

I wasn't sure how I'd be able to nod, stroke their heads, then let them go. I'd signed away any parental rights before they were born. Their mother's sister would have more legal standing than me, despite me being their birth father. Maybe they'd want to go with her. They'd only been with me for a lunar cycle, but they'd known her all their lives.

"Real like the game pieces feel alive?" Molly asked, walking down the hall beside Telsar while Curron and I followed. "Or it's so much fun they feel real."

"They're really alive," he said. "You'll see."

She shot me a glance full of amusement before laying her arm across Telsar's shoulder. He didn't shrug her away. If anything, he leaned into her, enjoying her touch.

That wrecked me too.

I was falling in love with her and so were my sons. Under normal circumstances, I could see me and Molly continuing to grow closer. I'd ask her to be my mate, and the boys would cheer when we told them. She'd say yes, of course. Or I hoped she would.

We dragged chairs over to the table where we'd play the game, and I retrieved it from the safe where I left it for safe-keeping. It was too tempting to be left out in the room.

When I dropped the big game box onto the table, the boys wiggled in their seats in excitement, and Molly's eyes widened.

"It takes up the entire table," she said.

I rubbed Curron's shoulder. "It sure does."

I lifted the lid off, revealing the players and gameboard.

"Yay, yay," Curron cried, shifting on his seat. His feet didn't reach the floor, and I was struck again by how young they still were. I wasn't sure if they'd remember their mother for long, and once they left here, they wouldn't remember me.

Tomorrow morning, I'd go into town and speak with the elders. After I explained, I'd ask them to intervene. I could only hope they'd feel my side was just, and that they'd state Daphne's sister couldn't take them away from me.

I sat and explained how the game was played, then waved to the board. "Pick your piece."

"They're in here," Curron said, tapping the square box in the center of the board. At his touch, the four sides of the lid sprang open, and four gamers leaped out to stand on each side of the roof.

Molly grinned. "Wow. I've never seen anything like this before."

"I want blue," Curron said. He looked up at me with so much pleading in his eyes, I'd give him the world if I could. "Can I have blue, Baji? Please?"

"Maybe Molly wants blue," I said.

Curron sagged in his seat and all the wind left his voice. "If she wants it, she can have it."

"I want the yellow one," Molly said.

"Baji always gets the yellow," Telsar said with a sneer, his snootiness restored. He tried to pluck it from her, but she held it high, giggling.

He snarled and left his chair, but as he stormed around toward her, she leapt up and raced across the room, holding the yellow game piece aloft.

He took off after her.

She flew around to the back of the sofa and stopped, grinning.

He stomped one way, then the next, but she kept moving. Frustration poured from him until she started laughing.

He looked horribly offended for a second before he started laughing too.

She raced around the sofa, scooped him up, and flopped on the cushions with him. "Who likes tickles?" Before he could say a word, she started teasing his belly. His rough laughter echoed around us, and he started tickling her too. Soon, they tumbled around on the floor like culair pups.

Me and Curron looked at each other, both of us trying to appear dignified, as if this type of roughhousing was beneath us.

We couldn't hold ourselves back for long. Soon, we were laughing along with them until tears streamed from our eyes.

"Should we break them up?" I asked Curron.

"Let's let them finish."

"Wise," I said, rubbing his shoulder.

"I like Molly," Curron told me. "Can we keep her?"

25
MOLLY

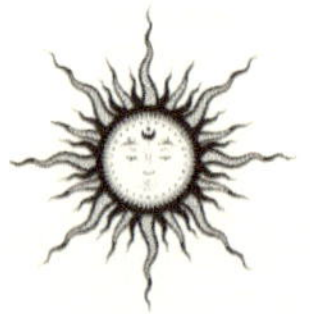

After playing the game, we took the boys upstairs, helped them clean their fangs and dress in PJs, and tucked them into bed.

"A story?" Curron asked with a yawn.

"Yes, please?" Telsar chimed in.

Something had changed between us, as if our tickling session had chased away any bad feelings. I wasn't sure if his new acceptance of me would hold, but I sensed he'd slide back and forth, spending more and more time in the boy he was after we returned to the game, one who truly smiled my way and seemed to like me. One day, maybe he'd stay there all the time.

As for a story, how could I resist his plea, let alone Curron's sleepy smile?

Firoh hovered in the doorway, listening. I was uncomfortable at first. Like, what did he think about my gargoyle tale? Winged creatures who lurked on buildings, turning to stone, didn't seem to be an alien thing. But he kept grinning during the funny parts, and I soon relaxed and got into the story.

I was so into it; I didn't realize that Telsar and Curron had fallen asleep. Ha. Rising from the chair I'd place between their beds, I made sure they were covered and crept to the doorway.

Firoh eased to the side to let me pass, though my body brushed against his. Heat climbed through me like a flame zipping along a line of gunpowder, aiming for the explosion at the end.

It was getting harder to hold back my growing feelings for him. I was going to crash hard if he wasn't interested in me any longer.

We shut their door and crept down the hall, taking the stairs to the lowest level and walking into the living area like we did each night. His limp seemed more pronounced. Did it hurt? I wanted to ask what happened, but felt he'd share if he wanted.

He poured me a drink, and we sat on the sofa, our sides and thighs touching.

Emotions churned through me. My growing affection for Firoh. My sadness over the boys' aunt wanting to take them away. And my enjoyment of life within this colony.

"Until tomorrow, I'm going to forget about their aunt," he said, holding up his glass and studying the pale pink liquid. "That's soon enough to worry."

"I think that's a great idea. You need a good night's sleep. That'll give you the strength to handle whatever comes next."

"I'm sure you're worried too."

I was, but I wouldn't add my burden to his. He had enough to deal with already.

We sipped our drinks, staring at the flames of the pseudofire he lit in the bowl sitting on the table between us. It was so realistic, as if my finger would burn if I ran it through the flames. It generated heat, but no smoke and it wouldn't burn, while still giving the comforting glow people had enjoyed for many generations.

He rubbed his thigh and couldn't hide his wince.

"You look sore," I said.

His hand stilled. "I was injured yaros ago. The wounds have healed, but it still pains me. It slows me. I hate that it holds me back."

"I'm sorry. I can't imagine having something like that happen."

"You're wounded yourself."

I'd wondered if he'd bring up the fact that I could no longer have children. "My wounds were fairly simple, though they had drastic consequences." I pressed my fist against my chest. "I hurt here now. Nowhere else."

"I'm sorry."

I shrugged and struggled not to cry. I thought I'd put this behind me.

"I shouldn't have mentioned it," he said.

Looking up at him, I took in his face filled with stoicism. He was so much like me. "Maybe I shouldn't have mentioned your leg."

"I don't mind." He also pressed his fist against his chest. "My true wounds will remain in my heart for the rest of my dias too." He sucked in a deep breath and released it. "How can my injuries compare to the loss of my agency partner?"

"What happened? You don't need to share if you don't want to," I hurried to add.

"I want to tell you. You understand. You've suffered physical loss and carry that wound in addition to the emotional one inside your heart." Firoh's eyes remained downcast; his face was a mask of grief and what I believed could be guilt. He ran his hand over his right leg and sighed heavily. As his hand moved, the fabric outlined ridges of scarred flesh beneath.

He looked up, his voice quiet and heavy with pain. "We were on a spy mission, me and my partner. We'd been tracking our target for days, but something went wrong. An ambush. My partner was killed, and I . . . I was wounded." He paused and his face cratered with grief as the memories washed over him. Did he live it over and over again?

"It's horrible, isn't it?" I did the same exact thing. He was an alien, a species different from humans, yet inside, we were very much the same.

"Truly, it is." He gritted his teeth and tried to force back the tears shimmering in his eyes. "The wounds were so bad I thought I would die. But I didn't. I survived while he died immediately in the explosion. Ever since, I've been living with what happened. I dream about it—nightmares, actually—and I'm reminded each time I take a step. Whenever pain shoots through my leg, I remember he's gone, that there must've been something I could've done to keep it from happening. I can never forget the fact that he died while I survived."

I leaned into his side, looking up at him, wishing I could help ease the agony he was living with.

"My wounds may have healed," he said softly, "but the knowledge that I could've done something, anything, will always linger. I hope one day I can learn to forgive myself."

"Was it really your fault?"

He shook his head, and a grim smile twisted his lips before they smoothed. "Not at all. He was the one who did the groundwork. I joined him to help complete the mission. He assured me he'd disarmed all the mines, that we'd be able to enter the hidden room in the compound and break up the interstellar drug ring's main headquarters."

"He missed one of the mines."

"Yeah."

"Whose job was it to make sure he didn't miss them?"

"The agency is always short staffed. Budget cuts and some nations refusing to pay their dues. We work for everyone throughout the universes, but without proper funding, we're—we *were*, that is, since I'm no longer with the agency—we were always struggling to complete a job."

"Lack of funding can kill." My words might sound harsh, but they were the truth.

"This is also why I quit. My boys are part of the reason, but I couldn't keep doing it. Maybe because I'm getting older."

"How old are you?"

"Thirty-one. Better to let young, enthusiastic agents handle things."

"While it's true that people slow down as they age, thirty-one *is* young."

"Not for that job."

Probably. He'd know. "I hope you can find a way to forgive yourself. We can only try. Sometimes we slip despite our best intentions."

He nodded, and I hoped he found a way to forgive himself.

I could understand blaming oneself. "My daughter died for no apparent reason, yet I still think there must've been something I did to make it happen."

"Had you fallen or anything like that?"

"No. I went for a regular check-up, and she was already gone. They didn't know why or when. They said these things can happen despite the best medical care."

"I'm sorry. Having my younglings here has shown me how precious they are, how much I want them in my life. I hate the thought of losing them, though they would be with family at least."

"Since losing my child, I wake up at night, thinking I hear her crying, that she needs me. Other times, I dream I'm holding her, that she was born and is with me. I feel so much joy. Then I realize it was just a dream, and I lose her all over again."

He put his arm around me. "Life can be cruel."

"And wonderful. I guess that's why people say we need to savor each moment. We really don't know how long anything will last."

What about him and me? I felt like we were growing closer, that we were building something lasting. Yes, life could snatch it away, but we still had now.

I didn't want to wait for the boys' aunt to arrive and wreck our little family. I wanted to show Firoh that what we had could support us through whatever might come next.

The moon rose slowly, but I didn't want to go to bed. I felt like my time with Firoh would end before I had a chance to fill my heart to overflowing. Only then could I cling to the memories of good times, remembering when I reached a low point in my life.

"What are you thinking about?" Firoh asked softly, placing his half-full glass on the table next to the pseudofire.

I shrugged. "About a lot of things." How could I share when so much of my thoughts were snagged with feelings?

I was falling in love with him, and he could be snatched out of my hands. They say loss makes you stronger, but I didn't want to test myself again. Not now. Not ever.

"What are *you* thinking?" I asked, turning on the sofa to face him. He was so much bigger than me. So different. Yet we fit together nicely. I couldn't imagine being with anyone else.

"I'm thinking about you, Molly." His deep voice sounded full of promises, but I could be reading him wrong. "With so much upheaval in my life, you give me joy, a reason to keep going."

"It's funny how life will take then give, isn't it?"

He nodded. "I've tried to stay away from you. Tell me right now if I'm stepping out of line, but I like you more than I should."

"I like you, Firoh." More than like actually. My mind spun. I'd never expected our conversation to head in this direction, but why wouldn't it? We'd shared a lot already. I was falling in love with him. Did he feel the same?

"I want you," he said with a groan. "Whatever you're willing to give."

26

FIROH

I held my breath, waiting for her to speak. With my son's aunt coming to claim them tomorrow, I could lose the younglings I'd grown to love.

But losing Molly would be just as devastating.

I'd told myself I should wait to speak with her after tomorrow, but how could I? I needed her in my life whether my sons remained here or not. If I didn't speak, she'd leave either with them or soon after, and I'd never know if reaching out to her could completely change my world.

"I want you, Firoh," she said, staring up at me with caring in her eyes. It made my breathing seize.

I gathered her into my arms and held her. My emotions were wild things right now. My true mate bond kept surging within me, but it was so much more than that. She was the one person I'd need for the rest of my life.

Leaning back, I stared down at her, memorizing her face like I'd done with my younglings every time I could since I learned I might lose them. I wanted to imprint each second I had with them before they left my life forever.

I wanted to do the same thing with Molly, make this moment and the next, and the one after that, count.

I cupped her face. "From the moment you came into my life, everything felt right. Speaking from my heart might scare you away, but I feel like I should. You need to know this, Molly. I'm falling in love with you."

"Firoh," she sighed and for one secunda, I thought she was going to reject me. Instead, she climbed onto my lap, spreading her legs around me. "I feel the same way. After my prior experience, I should be running in the other direction. But I don't want to leave you. I'm a whole person. Don't get me wrong there. But you make me feel more complete, as if you take my acceptable, uneven edges, and smooth them out. Polish them so they gleam."

How could I do anything other than kiss her? I captured her mouth with a kiss that made need spark inside me. Our mouths moved together in harmony. Being with Molly was like sliding into the calmest, warmest pool. Like life was balmy, fresh, and full of every sensation.

But being with her was also like stepping into the sea during a storm. My heart raced, and I drank in the beauty of the wonder within Molly. Her soul called me like a sirenest from the deep in the purest voice. I'd never want to hear another.

I kissed her neck, across her jaw, and the nape of her neck. She gasped, and I knew I was right where I wanted to be.

Emotion overwhelmed me. I wanted to touch her everywhere, as if my hands couldn't get enough of her soft skin.

I tugged lightly on the hem of her shirt, watching her face, unsure how far she wanted to take this. I could give her pleasure like before, or we could take this farther.

My sons were good about sleeping through the night,

and we were alone otherwise in my home, but still. I treasured her and wouldn't do anything to cause her regret.

My hands traveled up the curve of her back and down to the hem of her shirt. Our eyes locked together as if they were trying to capture all that we felt in this one moment.

I slid my fingers under the fabric, tugging it slowly over her head until she was left in only a simple garment restraining her breasts. Goosebumps raced across Molly's skin as my fingers grazed across her breasts through the material. Her nipples formed hard buds.

The craving for more of her body nearly took my breath away as our mouths met once again.

I continued to stroke her breasts through her garment, and she gasped against my mouth and shifted closer, pressing herself against me.

Everything about her was perfect. How had I been so fortunate to find her?

I slowly removed her undergarment, relishing the feel of her curves under my hands. Intensity beyond anything I'd ever experienced filled me as I began to kiss and lightly suck on each nipple, her gasps telling me I sent shockwaves of desire through her body. The feel of her skin . . . Her nipples. They hardened to ripe buds, and I couldn't get enough.

Gasping for air, Molly's eyes fluttered shut. She bit her lip and dug her fingernails into my sides as she enjoyed this moment between us.

My heart raced and desire flooded through me like the river behind my home when the spring rains arrived. Knowing that she wanted me just as much as I wanted her made my heart flip around in my chest.

Turning, I laid her on the cushions and took in how

beautiful she was, how she gazed up at me with heady longing.

I caressed her curves, watching her face, then leaned over and sucked her nipple into my mouth, running my tongue across it over and over. She writhed, breathing heavily while arching her hips up toward me.

Watching her face, I undid the fastener on her pants and slid the fabric down her hips. She kicked them aside.

I kissed across her belly, stroking between her legs. She parted her thighs and urged me on with her moans.

She was incredibly wet, and I nearly came right then, but I would hold on and make sure she experienced everything wonderful. She deserved this, and I was grateful I could give it to her.

I ran the pad of my thumb down her slit, and she thrust up toward my hand.

"You like this," I said.

"Yes, Firoh. Don't stop."

Parting her thighs further, I moved down her body, kissing the soft curve of her belly and the tops of her thighs. I trailed my lips inward, aiming for her heady scent. I needed to taste her. Now.

Finding her clit, I rolled the tender bud. She groaned and thrust her hips up.

Holding her down with my other hand, I licked her, savoring how wonderful she felt on my tongue, how she tasted.

She was wild beneath me, and I loved it. Giving her joy like this made me feel complete.

"You're going to come for me," I growled.

"Yes," she whispered. "I need you. Need that."

I nipped and licked her sensitive flesh, my claws grazing lightly against her hardened bud. My other hand roamed her body, lightly scraping her sensitive skin. She shuddered and quaked with pleasure as I explored her inner depths with my tongue, tasting her sweet wetness. I pushed it further and deeper, bringing her closer and closer to the edge of ecstasy.

Her hands clutched my hair, tugging and pulling.

That nearly drove me over the edge. I'd never realized how sensitive my hair could be to a lover's touch.

Mate. My linked mate. The flare across my skin at our first meeting told me she was mine, but her responses each time we touched solidified it in my mind.

I pushed my tongue into her with her cries of pleasure filling the air. Her body began to vibrate with an impending orgasm, and I wanted to wring every bit of pleasure out of her.

"Firoh! Yes, oh, yes. Please." Her hips rose to meet my tongue. Her eyelids closed as she gave over to the sensations wracking her body.

I loved that I could do this for her. With so much sadness in our lives, we needed moments like this to refill us.

That's what Molly did for me. She took my scraps of sadness and fused them back together. I wasn't whole, but I was so much better than when I was without her.

I drove my tongue inside her harder, adding fingers with retracted claws, stretching her. She was tight and wet, and I couldn't get enough of her taste and her moans.

She gave way all at once, tensing before crying out hoarsely, her body shuddering. Her inner walls milked my tongue and fingers, spasming.

With a groan, she collapsed beneath me.

27
MOLLY

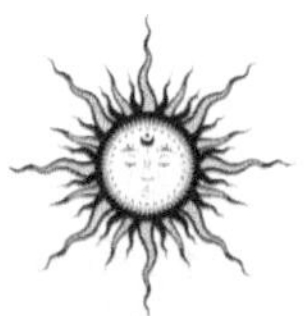

I'd never experienced anything like Firoh's touch in my life. I'd been married, for heaven's sake. I'd believed I loved my husband. Yet I'd never felt the same connection with Tyler that I did with Firoh each time we came together, and we hadn't even had full sex.

"I want you," he said, rising over me. "This moment. Tomorrow. And for as long as you want to give yourself to me. Be my forever mate. My *linked* mate. My always."

"That's so beautiful, Firoh," I said, wrapping my arms around his shoulders. "Be my forever mate. My linked mate. My always."

"Mate," he said softly, his voice croaking with joy. He grinned and released a growl, nibbling on my neck and breasts until the tickle made me giggle.

We sobered quickly, though smiles still teased across our mouths.

"Would you like to go upstairs?" he asked.

"Separate bedrooms?"

His head tilted as he watched my face. "If you insist."

"What if I insist on sharing yours?"

"I will never turn down that offer."

He helped me dress, and we slunk up the stairs, trying to keep our steps quiet to keep from waking the boys.

Sweeping open his door, he lifted me and took me inside the darkness, turning to shut the panel. He pressed me against it with a growl and kissed me until I was a moaning wreck all over again. I'd just had an amazing orgasm, but I had a feeling I'd soon experience more.

He didn't turn on a light but carried me across the room and dropped into a chair near the window. Outside, the stars shone, bright and clear, one of the first things I noticed the night we caught loogots. The moon was brighter here without city lights muting its glow, and the stars felt so big and close, I could almost reach up and touch them.

"I want to take you to my bed and love you all night," he said. "But I want to hold you first and tell you how much you mean to me. When I met you, heat flared up my arms. This means only one thing among my people. You're my linked mate, my precious one, Molly."

"That's what you meant by us being linked." I grinned, loving this. "I've read books where the couple was fated mates. Is it something like that?"

"We are fated to be," he said solemnly. "I feel this in my heart. I will adore you for the rest of my days. I chose to give into the linked mate glow, though I believe my heart would recognize you no matter where or when I found you."

His tail wrapped around my waist and stroked along my neck. The tip was soft yet smooth, almost rubbery. He watched me, and with the moon shining bright, there was enough light I could see his expression. His skin reflected the light, and while I'd never thought a guy with purple skin could be attractive, I wouldn't have him any other way. He was my Firoh, my linked mate. I knew this in my heart as strongly as him. Humans may not bond in the same way as his species, but I was fated to belong to him.

His eyes blazed with a deep hunger that sent a shiver through my body. I'd never felt anything like this before, this nearly overwhelming sensation coursing through my veins and setting my heart racing. I was at a turning point in my life, and with Firoh holding my hand, we'd walk into the future together. I'd help him reconcile his feelings about the loss of his partner, and he'd help me heal from the loss of my daughter.

I was drawn to him, the urge to take him into my heart and body nearly overwhelming. I wanted to explore this new, heady emotion he drove within me and feed it back to him until his heart was bursting.

I slowly removed my clothes, then helped him out of his. I urged him into a chair and climbed onto him, strad-dling him.

His tail stroked from my neck to my breast, where it teased across one nipple then the other, bringing both to hard nubs.

Our eyes locked, and a wave of desire washed over me. I couldn't deny the need to be closer to him any longer.

I leaned forward, brushing my skin against his. He curled toward me and captured my lips, just like he was quickly capturing my heart.

Sensations flooded me, and passion made me lift, rubbing against his stiff cock. It seemed bigger than any I'd taken before, but I sensed it would give me the best plea-sure of my life. Not just because it had stiff rings along the sides, but because it was Firoh's.

Heat flushed my skin, and my breathing came in ragged

gasps. I stroked his chest as his tail curled around behind me.

As I massaged his arms and teased his nipples, he slipped the tip of his tail between my legs.

I stilled, and he looked down at me, his eyes filled with need.

He watched me as the end of his tail carefully explored my folds, dipping through my wetness.

When he teased the tip across my clit and then slid it a fraction inside me, he stilled. "Yes or no?"

He'd do whatever I wished. I controlled this interaction. If I wasn't comfortable, he wouldn't push or judge me. He'd smile and care for me just the same.

That was freeing, and a boldness filled me, urging me on.

"Yes," I whispered, watching him as intently as he did me.

He pushed his tail inside me. It wasn't as large as his cock, but that might be a good thing. I needed to warm up a bit, though the thought of him using his cock was making my bones sing.

I lifted and dropped as he moved his tail within me.

He tilted my face up, and our eyes locked. "I want to watch you come. Will you do that for me?"

"I will." With others, it might make me feel vulnerable, but not with Firoh.

He chuckled, low and sexy. "Come from my tail, and I'll make sure you do the same with my cock. I want you so much. It makes me feel scared. I don't want to lose you."

I grabbed his shoulders. "I won't betray you or leave you." Perhaps it was a mistake to give him everything, to lay myself bare to whatever might be thrown our way next, but it felt right.

As his tail moved within me, my fingers trailed across his skin, exploring each ridge of muscle. If only I could memorize this wonderful feeling of being in his arms, of now. Freeze it in case I needed it later.

He watched me, and I let my pleasure show on my face. In the past, it had been hard to let myself go completely, to give into the moment and the sensations shooting through my body without being aware of how the other person might be feeling.

He grinned. "I love this."

"You've got a raging hard-on," I said with a laugh. "I'm the one having fun."

"Oh, it's fun. Never doubt that." He tilted his head. "What if I do this?"

Something started buzzing against my clit. A glance down showed the head of his cock pressing against it, sliding across it as I moved.

"You know many would kill to have a vibrating cock?"

"It's yours. You'll take it soon. Now stop distracting yourself. Let yourself go. Enjoy this so I can enjoy it too."

I grinned. "It's a deal."

When I focused only on his tail moving within me and the head of his cock hitting my clit, pleasure burst inside me. I kissed his chest and tipped my head back, riding him wildly.

He curled forward and kissed me.

Moaning, I pressed against him. When I leaned into him, lifting and dropping faster, he increased the pace of his tail, pushing it deep.

Our kiss deepened, each of us savoring the sensations flooding through us. I clung to him as I moved, pushing down hard against his tail. His hands explored my body, teasing, then rolling my nipples, making moans burst from deep within me.

His lips moved hungrily against mine. Our kiss was full of longing and need, and pressure built inside me. I was going to erupt soon and there was no stopping it.

My orgasm shot through me suddenly, and I broke away from our kiss, releasing a guttural groan.

His gaze locked on mine. "Yes. It's beautiful. You're gorgeous. My mate. My only one."

I continued to quiver, still holding his eyes. I'd never felt this complete before. This treasured.

He stood and carried us over to the bed, his tail slipping out of my body. Dropping onto the surface, he held me, his hands gliding along my back in long strokes.

"I think I've found nirvana," I said.

When he wasn't sure what I meant, I explained.

"Maybe I'm the one who has found complete and utter peace," he said.

I stroked his cock. "With this hard thing?"

"Well, I *am* aware of it." His voice went growly from my touch.

"Then let me see what I can do about it, okay?" I said with a grin.

I shifted my position. When I sucked the head of his cock into my mouth, he lifted his hips and groaned.

So I sucked in some more.

28

FIROH

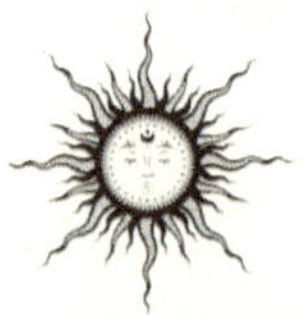

My heart raced as she kissed the most sensitive part of my body, her wet lips sending delicious shocks of pleasure through me. As if every nerve in my body was suddenly alive, every inch of skin became a sensitive point for her to explore.

She moved up and down, taking my cock deep within her mouth. Humming, she stroked her tongue across me. Her mouth was a smooth glove, holding me with just the right amount of pressure. I gasped as she pulled me deeper. Her fingers stroked the rest of my length and my balls.

"Molly," I said, gliding my fingers through her hair and across her face.

Her mouth moved on me, and I could tell she was grinning. She enjoyed doing this as much as I savored the gift she was giving.

Like a youngling during his first time, my body tensed, ready to let loose. My muscles tightened, and every exhale became a groan. Heat coiled inside me, but I couldn't bear to pull away long enough to bury myself within her body.

All I could do was lay back and feel; overcome with how amazing this was.

One of her hands held my cock steady while the other caressed my legs and abdomen, her fingertips exploring the contours of my body with the same eagerness and care as she gave my cock. She glided them over my scars, giving that wounded part of me equal, loving attention.

Her tongue and mouth kept moving up and down my length, and she whispered gentle words against my skin. I couldn't focus on anything else. Just my hunger and need and how lovingly she gave this moment to me.

My body trembled, and my heart pounded with anticipation. I stroked her hair and neck, my fingers caressing her soft skin. My muscles tensed, and full shakes took over my body.

It wasn't possible for me to love her more than I did in this moment. She was a gift to me from the fates, one I would hold close and protect for the rest of my dias.

"I'm gonna . . ."

She hummed again, nodding, and that was all it took.

I shot everything I had inside her mouth.

29
MOLLY

Nothing made me happier than feeling the joy bursting inside him.

Leaving his cock with a pop of my mouth, I climbed up his body and draped myself across him. His arms went around me, and his breathing slowed.

"That . . ." He shook his head. His tail coiled around me, and I decided I wanted it wrapped around my waist forever. We could figure out how to walk around and do things during the day like that, right?

I must've fallen asleep because I woke at dawn to his fingers stroking me. As if he sensed I was awake, his touch deepened, the glide of his palms becoming longer and more heated. He kept sliding his fingers near my breasts, but never touching. And his sly tail had left my waist and was teasing between my legs. When I parted my thighs, it dove between them, finding my clit in a flash.

My groan slipped out, and he rolled me onto my back. Braced over me, he grinned.

"I was beginning to think I was going to have to wake you up," he said.

"No sleeping in for me, huh?" I said with a laugh.

His mood sobered. "It was wonderful holding you all night. And what you did for me . . . No one has done that before. Your warmth and caring made every thought fly from my mind. I want you forever, but I'm not going to pressure you. We've just begun our journey together, and it's right that we wait to see where the next path takes us before doing more."

Truly, though, you could never tell what might happen next. Look at us. Yesterday, the world was spread out before us. Today, we had to worry the boys' aunt would take them away.

I didn't want to think about that now, though. This moment was for me and Firoh.

"I want to love you fully, my linked mate," he said, his gaze locked on mine.

I loved how he sought permission, but didn't he know he could sometimes take?

"Love me," I whispered, needing him already. What we'd found together could never be replicated with someone else. It was special, and as I'd already suspected, lasting.

He kissed me, soon leaving my lips to feather kisses along my jaw. My neck got equal attention before he reached my breasts.

While he sucked one nipple into his mouth, then the other, his tail slid between my legs, gliding across my clit before dipping inside me just enough to make me wet but never quite bringing me to a splintering finish.

When I thought I was going to shatter from his touch, he shifted backward, kissing across my belly before parting my thighs. He moved between them, grinning up at me.

"You taste amazing, and I need to eat breakfast. You're alright with that, I assume?"

Ready to come already, all I could do was nod.

He licked up my slit, then dipped his warm, long tongue inside me, gliding it across my inner walls. His tail focused on my clit, shifting back and forth, alternating the rhythm to drive me out of my mind.

I was shooting across the stars, tasting them. The fullness of the universe spread around me. Nothing existed but this moment with Firoh. I felt more alive than I ever had. My skin tingled, and my heart pounded in my ears.

Lost in his touch and the feel of his mouth and tail between my legs, I didn't care if I ever emerged.

When I thought I'd give way and shoot beyond the farthest stars, he rose above me. "Hold onto that for me, will you? I want to feel you come around my cock." His fingers glided along my sides, and his tail kept running through my wetness, keeping me on the crest of something amazing.

It was so freeing to be able to joke with him about something like this. Who would've thought I'd find someone who mirrored my soul?

"Unless you'd rather get up and get dressed?" he said, a sly grin filling his face.

"Never."

He flipped me over onto my belly and lifted my hips. "I'm going to ride you until you scream at least eight times."

"Make it ten and it's a deal." Damn, I was bold. I loved it.

From the growl he released, so did he.

He placed the head of his cock at my opening, and I

spread my legs wider. I'd seen his cock. Tasted it and licked it. I'd taken as much of it into my mouth as I could, and that had only been half.

Shifting his hips forward, he dipped the vibrating head of his cock inside me. Damn, that felt good. My moan ripped out, and he leaned over me to nibble on my shoulders.

"Can I make you come before me?" he asked pleasantly, like we were walking in the woods.

"I dare you to try." I pressed my grinning face into the mattress. I'd gotten used to these mattresses that felt like a mix of memory foam and some sort of living sponge. The sponginess didn't suck at my body as much as cushion it. I sunk in in the right places but never felt like I would drown. I woke each morning after the best sleep of my life.

Although sleeping with Firoh only made it better.

He shifted forward, burying more of his cock inside me. Yeah, it was big, but it seemed my body could take it.

"All of it," I barked. Look at me. A timid woman now making sexual demands.

"Not so soon. Time for you to come."

Yeah, like that was going to happen without him driving into me?

Something started vibrating inside me. Oh, yeah, the head of his cock. The sensation reverberated through my bones and snapped back to focus on my clit. How was he directing where the vibration went?

It didn't matter. My body sucked down the feeling and like whiplash, drove me over the edge.

I groaned as I came.

He chuckled. "Keep milking my cock, little one. I need it."

How could a woman growl at a guy who savored making her come eight or ten times before him?

"One down," he said. "Time to build another." He pushed forward, still not giving me all his length.

Finally, he seated himself fully. He paused, waiting for my body to adjust.

"Amazing," I whispered.

He grunted and started moving slowly.

His tail coiled around me and stroked my clit, and in no time, heat spiraled inside me again. He might be right about multiples. Just because no one else had ever taken the time to make sure I was as into it as him didn't mean all guys were like that.

His pace increased, as did the movements of his tail. I coiled tight and released, each time nearly coming apart.

When another hit me, it was both sweet and hot, a surge from deep within me. I gasped, and he started moving faster, riding along with me as my body peaked and slid down the other side.

My eyes had rolled back in my head. I began to wonder if eight was too many orgasms at once. But before I could say anything, my body smoothed out and started climbing the hill all over again.

A gasping wreck, I moved against him, widening my legs and urging him on with furious pants and whimpers.

I was on fire, and I no longer wondered if I could handle this. Oh, hell, yeah, I could. This and so much more.

"More," I whispered, cresting before sliding back. Did I have it in me? We'd see. My body begged for the release I knew waited for us both.

I trembled with anticipation rising and crashing once more. Three? Or was that four? I'd lost count, and I no longer cared. All I could focus on was the feel of him moving inside me and the vibrating head of his cock. He directed it to different areas, and I'd never realized there were so many different erogenous zones inside my pussy. Each of his thrusts brought me further and further into a pleasure so intense I thought I would never come back.

I shot all the way to the top again, and my moan echoed around us. I was a quivering wreck, but Firoh kept going, slowing to give my body time to rest before picking up the pace again and pushing me to give more.

Losing track of everything else, I gave myself over to him. Trust was not easily given, but this guy held my heart in his tender embrace. He'd never hurt me.

When I'd given all I could, and he'd wrung every emotion and feeling from my body, he came with a heavy groan. We collapsed together on the bed; him shifting me around until I could lay across his chest.

I couldn't think of anything he could offer that would make me feel more complete than I did in this moment. I hoped it never ended, that what we'd built would sustain us through whatever might come.

He stroked my hair. "I want to tease you about how many times you came, but numbers don't really matter. You've given me the greatest gift, mate. Your body, your heart, and your soul. With you, I'm complete."

I kissed his chest, barely having the energy to lift my upper body enough to meet his eyes. "I never knew it could be like this, that I'd feel this close to someone while making love."

Rising, he gave me a kiss. "It will only get better."

I'd trust in that. In us.

We gave each other tender kisses until the stars faded and early morning shadows filled the sky.

I felt a deep peace, knowing that we'd experienced

something beautiful and intense, something I would never forget. What we'd shared was new and wonderful. As perfect as life could offer.

30
FIROH

Time stood still, like I was dreaming. More sensations than I could handle coursed through me.

An intense need to protect my mate. That came from my species and the linked bond we'd formed.

Longing to make this female happy at all times. I wasn't sure how I'd do that because life could suck. But I was going to try.

Love.

My love for Molly is like a rivalarn flower blooming in the months after the long cold. When I was around her, I felt so full I could burst with joy. She'd captivated my soul with her kindness, and I was completely entranced.

All night, I reminded myself of how lucky I was to have her with me. No matter what came next, she would be the stability I would cling to. She was my light in the darkness, and my love for her shone brighter than any star in the night sky.

Dawn came, and the sun rose with red and orange light bleeding across the sky. I slipped from our bed and stood at the window, watching the glowing orb lumber up into the sky. Clouds formed, coating the sun, and I could tell the day would be overcast. Grim.

It would suit what would come next.

I had no legal standing with my younglings, and that was eating me apart. How could I say goodbye when I'd only recently found them? I loved them, and I would all my days. The thought of not being a part of their life left me feeling bereft, as if a big chunk of my heart was about to be ripped out and tossed aside.

What could I do? I'd appeal to the elders, but I wasn't confident they'd decide in my favor or that they'd go against the universal council.

"Time to get up?" Molly asked sleepily from the bed.

I left the dawn and whatever it might bring and crossed the room, stopping beside the bed. "Stay in bed. Sleep." She'd been so lush and giving; I was unable to resist. Her tiny body had accommodated my needs more than anyone I'd ever been with. I was still stunned by how wonderful it had been.

She tossed back the blankets. "I need to work with the boys."

I tugged them back up over her and gave her a kiss. "I'll make breakfast. I . . . is it alright if I spend some time with them this morning?" I couldn't name the words haunting us both, that it might be the last time I'd be with them. "They can skip lessons today."

"Of course. I'll see you all at lunchtime?" She stifled a yawn and gave me a soft smile. "Do you have specific plans?"

"You mentioned fishing when you arrived. I thought I'd take them to the river and let them try to catch our meal. I imagine they'll spend more time splashing in the water, but it'll be fun to watch them." It would hurt. So much. "I want to make a few memories." Ones I could cling to after they were gone.

Molly climbed out of the bed and wrapped her arms around me, pressing her cheek against my chest. "I'm sorry. I wish I had a solution for this horrible situation."

I did too, but I didn't believe one would be found.

"After we're done, I need to go into town," I said. "I'll speak with the elders before my younglings' aunt arrives." I couldn't take my boys with me, though I was going to have to explain what was happening before their aunt arrived late today.

"I'll make the time you're gone to town fun too," she said, looking up at me.

If only this was a regular day, I'd take her back to bed and love her until my younglings were knocking on the door, telling me it was time to get up. We'd make breakfast together, laughing, and plan our dia. One dia like this would stretch into another and keep going after that, each full of sunshine and love.

"I barely started building this life, and I'm about to lose it." I hated burdening Molly with my pain, but I wanted to share.

"I understand. I've come to love them. I hate that I won't be with them as they grow up."

Moving to Earth might be an option. Would Molly be open to that idea? I'd wait to speak with the elders before bringing it up. Surely, if their aunt was able to legally take them from me, she wouldn't deny me a place in their life.

31
MOLLY

I lounged in bed a bit, but once I was awake, I was one of those people who had to get the day going.

After bathing, I tidied the boys' room, sanitizing their dirty clothing and bedding, and made everything look fresh and inviting. While I did it, the shadow of their impending loss hung over me. I could be cleaning a room they'd never return to again.

It was all I could do not to cry. They'd wiggled their way into my heart. I hated that I could soon lose them.

It wasn't hard for me to see parallels to them being taken from us to the loss of my child. This wasn't about me, though. I wanted to be the support Firoh was going to need if his conversation with the elders didn't go as we'd like.

Downstairs, I tackled the kitchen, nibbling on the breakfast leftovers while I did it. Muted cries of joy echoed from down by the river, telling me the boys were having a great time with their dad. I was tempted to sneak down there and watch, but this was Firoh's time with them, and I wouldn't disturb it.

After that, I sat in the living area reading a holobook on

my wrist com. It wasn't hard to sink into the romance novel. I'd always loved reading about others finding their happy endings.

By the time the boys burst into the house with Firoh, their cheeks bright from the hazy sunshine and their eyes glowing with happiness, I'd made lunch.

We sat in the kitchen together, consuming it.

"You're a great cook," Firoh said after he'd eaten everything on his plate.

Heat rose in my face. I wasn't used to praise. "It's a simple dish."

"Take it from a trained chef. It was excellent."

"I liked it," Telsar said tentatively. "Will you make it again?"

I wanted to leap around and shriek with joy. He was truly warming up to me. I hoped it wasn't too late. I ruffled his hair. "I'll be happy to."

If only they'd still be here when I made it.

"Yummy," Curron said with a yawn.

"I was thinking we could do some lessons after lunch," I told them. "Your baji has to go into town for a meeting."

"I explained that I need to speak with the elders about some vital issues," Firoh said.

"Elders are boring," Telsar said. "I'd rather stay here. Can we do something fun, Molly?"

"Of course. We haven't been swimming yet." I looked Firoh's way. "Would it be okay for us to swim in the river? I haven't had the chance to ask if it's safe. The boys said they took swimming lessons back on Earth. If they don't have suits, we'll figure something out."

"The river's safe." His warm gaze traveled across me, and I sensed he was thinking about our night together and how wonderful it had been. "I believe they brought something that could be swimsuits with them. Look in their closet. I don't wear much when I swim, but I suppose Earthlings do."

Did he picture us swimming naked together? I'd suggest it later if we were up for something like that. So much depended on what happened with their aunt. I wouldn't feel up to doing anything if she took them. Would she give us time to adjust to the idea? This was all so sudden.

"I'll get going, then," Firoh said, rising. He took his dish to the sink and returned to the table. "I'll miss you," he told Curron as he kissed his forehead. "And you too, little one," he added to Telsar, who also received a kiss.

Curron, love bug that he was, drank it up. Telsar squirmed, but the happiness in his eyes told me he loved receiving his father's affection.

I assume their aunt loved them. Why else travel all this way to take them from their father? But ripping them from their dad's arms was going to cause harm that might never be soothed. In a way, they'd lose two parents in a very short time.

Firoh paused beside me and kissed my forehead. If he was like me, he'd love to do more. We were a couple now, and if Telsar and Curron miraculously remained with Firoh, we'd share the news with them. Until then, I was okay with sneaking around to be together.

I stroked his side as he left the room.

Telsar frowned my way but said nothing. Curron was busy trying to bury one of his spellons with his leftovers.

"Let's clean up and do some lessons so we can go swimming," I announced, rising to Curron's cheers. Telsar nodded and got up, hurrying to the sink with his plate.

We did the dishes, and I took the boys to the living area

where we sat and went through math and writing. The internal translator I'd had implanted a few years ago miraculously made me write their species' language and speak it flawlessly, though they could speak my language, having grown up on Earth. They could write decently already, and they told me about school back on Earth and mentioned their favorite teacher.

Maybe one day, the universal scientific labs would come up with a device they could implant that would replace teachers. If that information was available to your brain, you wouldn't need someone to show it to you.

That could be boring. There was joy in learning something new, in exploring the world around you, and in interacting with others while you learned.

After lunch, I had them read on their dashes—whatever they wanted, though their libraries were limited to age-appropriate books. I did the same, sinking into a monster romance. I just loved them. The one I was reading was about a human woman falling in love with a gargoyle. I kept laughing, which was good, though Telsar shot me a scowl.

Curron sat on the sofa next to me, leaning into my side, and Telsar took my other side. He watched my face when he did it, and while I wanted to grin, I held it back, merely nodding to show him he was welcome.

If only we had more time to stretch the bond forming between us.

"How about swimming?" I asked half an hour or so later. Firoh would be back from town soon, and while I was eager to hear what the elders had to say, he wouldn't want to speak in front of his sons. Not yet.

In their closet, I found swim trunks, and was grateful whoever packed their things included them.

I hadn't brought a suit, but one of the shirts I'd bought in town came to my mid-thigh, and with panties, that should be enough.

"Gonna have fun," Curron sang as we walked down the path to the river. "Goin' swimmin'!"

I sang, too, and though Telsar shot us both a rueful glance and he didn't sing, he did hurry along beside his brother. Was this his baseline or had he also been a sunny boy when he lived with his mom? It was sad that he held himself back all the time.

We tossed our drying cloths on the shore and stepped into the surprisingly warm water.

"Oh," I said with a shiver despite the balmy temp. I wasn't used to swimming. Bathing wasn't common either since water was rare in most places. Most people used cleansing units to remain clean. Some units even removed hair in whatever area you chose, though I'd never used one of those. Too expensive.

The boys leapt in, swimming farther out before turning to tread water. They were solid swimmers, which made my heartrate slow a bit from the furious rhythm it had picked up when they splashed in with complete abandon.

I joined them, paddling to the middle, and though I could easily touch bottom, I floated with my knees bent, dipping down into the water to my chin.

"This feels amazing," I said.

"I want to swim every day," Curron said.

"I think it gets cold here sometimes, and there might be storms, but on any warm, sunny day? I'll join you."

Curron swished his arm back and forth, creating growing ripples, and in no time, the younglings were splashing each other, hooting their joy.

Hearing them happy kept me grinning.

"Who wants to race?" Telsar cried out.

"Me, me," Curron shouted, his excitement mixing in with mine.

"We need to swim upriver," Telsar said. "Then we'll race until we're at the shore where we left our towels. First one there wins."

"I'm gonna win," Curron said, grinning my way. "Right, Molly?"

"You're an amazing swimmer," I said. "But so is Telsar. I saw how you did the breaststroke a few minue ago," I added to Telsar, who beamed.

"I . . . " He shook his head and whirled around, swimming upriver. "Let's go!"

What had he been about to say? I'd like to think it was something that would make my heart sing, but for all I knew, he'd been about to tell me he didn't want me to race with them. You could never tell with Telsar.

I remained behind them as they swam to keep an eye on them, but truly, they were great swimmers. When we'd rounded a bend and it got shallow, we turned.

"Let's take a breather," I said, though I wasn't puffing. Curron might want one, though.

"Ready?" Telsar asked, hopping around in the water.

A low hum rang out, but when I looked around, I didn't see a cause. I shrugged it off and focused on the upcoming event. I wouldn't truly race. Again, I'd watch over the boys. But I'd make sure Telsar thought I put in a good effort.

"On three," Telsar said when I nodded to show I was ready. He counted down, then splashed through the water, his legs kicking and his arms slicing along the surface.

Curron kept pace, and it was going to be a neck-and-neck finish with me coming in last.

We rounded the bend, and movement to my right

caught my eye. Someone was walking across the back lawn. Was Firoh back?

I swam harder to keep up with the boys, paying attention to them rather than the person approaching the shore.

We reached the towels, and the boys sprang up, leaping around with each other.

"I won," Curron crowed.

"No me," Telsar cried. "Molly, tell him that I—"

"Telsar? Curron?" someone called out from the top of the bank.

They stopped, then frowned and turned in her direction.

"Auntie Daphne?" Telsar shouted, his voice croaking. "Auntie Daphne!" He splashed toward shore, falling but getting back up with Curron right beside him.

They scrambled up the bank and raced into their aunt's outstretched arms.

32
FIROH

I arrived home when Daphne was trying to get my sons to climb into her transfer shuttle.

Molly fretted beside her, reaching in to hold Telsar's hand before grabbing Curron's.

Daphne appeared to have come alone, but that didn't stop me from stomping across my backyard and lifting my boys out of the interior of the three-person capsule. I backed away, lowering them to the ground and nudging them behind me. Molly remained with me, placing her arms around my younglings' shoulders.

"Excuse me," Daphne said in the same snooty voice I'd heard Telsar use too many times on Molly. She stomped toward me, waving her wrist com in the air. "I have everything here that states I have complete and full custody of these children. Take your hands off them and back away."

"Where is Auntie Daphne taking us?" Curron whimpered.

She stooped down and held out her arms. "Come to me, Curron. You too, Telsar. We're returning to Earth. I've missed you so much." Only the break in her voice and the obvious sorrow on her face kept me from growling. It was clear she adored them as much as me, which was going to be a problem.

"You do not have the authority to take them," Moonsten called out, walking as quickly as she could around the stem of my home and advancing toward us. She huffed up to stand with me, rubbing her lower back. "It would appear I've arrived just in time."

A low call from the front of my yard told me she'd ridden her culair here. It had taken me too much time to track her down and explain, and then she had wanted to notify the other elders before stating she would return here with me to confront Daphne. Few took on edicts handed down from the universal council, but she'd assured me she had jurisdiction here. She and the elders would confer and come to a final decision but it wouldn't be today.

"And who are you?" Daphne asked, straightening. Her hands flopped to her sides, and if they weren't trembling slightly, I'd read her as only angry from the tone of her voice.

Moonsten drew herself up, her chin lifting. "I am the senior elder of this colony, duly elected, and my rule is law."

Thuds rang out and Kreel came barreling around my house with his Xilan friend Wuldron right behind him. Kreel skidded to a stop beside me, his hair in disarray and his face ruddy. Wuldron flanked him, his hand on the large blade strapped to his waist.

Wuldron had moved to our colony not long ago, and we'd welcomed our first Xilan warrior. He'd built a home and kept to himself most of the time, which was the way most of us liked it.

"Got here as soon as one of the elders sent word," Kreel said.

"Boys," I said. "I want you to go sit on the table out front and wait for me there."

Telsar frowned. "But Baji—"

"Now. Please." I kept my voice as light as I could.

They left us, walking out front, though remaining within view. Hopefully well enough away they wouldn't hear what we said.

Wuldron's gaze swept the area, seeking threats. He'd served his government as a space commander, and there were few outside of him I'd rather have coming to my defense. His attention focused on Daphne, and a confused look appeared in his eyes. His tail swept back and forth, and his low huff rang out in the yard.

Xilans had one universal feature: a slaking. I watched the blue skin on his arms but didn't see any streaks that might indicate it was nearly upon him.

He dragged his gaze from Daphne and shook his head.

Daphne gaped at his reptilian skin and slitted, penetrating eyes. He had bluish scales and six-inch horns jutting from his long, thick bands of pale blue hair. Her eyes fell on the claws on his thumbs, and color rose into her face. She must've realized we saw her staring.

She recovered quickly. "And who are you?" Daphne asked Kreel and, to some extent, Wuldron.

My orc friend was an impressive sight, from his towering, muscular build to his tusks, to his often snarly demeanor. Wuldron was just as tall and muscular. Both must've been working in Kreel's field because mud coated their bare chests, boots, and pants.

"I am Kreelevar Nohmal Trirag Grikohr, Manager of this colony," my friend said. He flicked his hand toward Wuldron. "Wuldron."

A smile lifted Wuldron's lips for one secunda, revealing his fangs. "Wuldron Veskalonire Ambrosten, if you please."

"Daphne . . ." Her swallow took a long time going down. "Daphne Marstens Prentess. It's, um, nice to meet you." She stared at Wuldron for a long while.

His tail stiffened, and for a minue, I thought he was going to stalk right up to her. I wasn't sure what he'd do when he got there, but their entire interaction confused me.

"I have the universal council's ruling," Daphne said, her voice softening. She wrenched her gaze from Wuldron to the boys. "I'm their aunt. I was away on a job and out of wrist com reach when my sister . . ." Tears pooled in her eyes, and I saw hints of Curron in her face and mannerisms. "When my sister died."

Daphne blinked fast. "As soon as they tracked me down, I rushed back to Earth. By then, it was too late. The government had taken my nephews and sent them to some random space station." Her voice rose. "I came after them as soon as I could, only to find them gone from there and taken to a backwater colony far from Earth!"

"Backwater, huh?" Molly whispered. "Can't she see how wonderful this place is? I did from the moment I arrived."

I wanted to hug and kiss her for saying that. This was a great place to raise younglings. Just because Daphne couldn't see that didn't mean their lives here would be torture.

"You cannot stop me from taking my nephews," Daphne said. If her eyes weren't sparkling with tears and frustration, I'd snarl.

"I can, and I will," Moonsten said firmly, reinforcing her words with a tap of her cane on the ground.

"I know my rights," Daphne shrieked, waving her wrist com in the air. "The universal council said they were mine."

"If you try to circumvent my order," Moonsten said, "the universal council will never decide in your favor."

Daphne's lips twisted. "They'd have to find me. I've gotten good at hiding."

"Good enough to evade an interstellar interpol agent?" Kreel asked.

Wuldron grunted. "I wouldn't want one coming after me."

"Good luck finding someone to take on a job like that," Daphne said with a sneer.

"Seems I'm looking at one right now." Kreel's gaze fell on me.

Daphne frowned. "You're not..."

I nodded, a grim smile rising on my face. "Recently retired, but I've been an agent for longer than my younglings have been alive. If you think I won't find you and make sure you never see my boys again, try me."

She shuddered. "Alright. I'll await the elder's decision." Her gaze softened when she looked toward the boys. "I've missed them so much. I need them in my life."

"We are hosting a bake-off in town five dias from now," Moonsten said. "We will announce our decision after the event."

With that, she pivoted and took Kreel's arm, using his assistance to round the base of my home.

33
MOLLY

The boys raced back to us.

"You can't take us from Baji," Curron cried, clinging to my leg.

Telsar sniffed. "We love him. We want to stay here with Baji and Molly."

He'd squirm if I tried to kiss him, so I put my arm around his shoulders instead, tugging him close. He leaned into me, his eyes swimming with tears. Poor guy. He and his brother were being yanked in one direction after another. At this rate, they'd never feel secure.

Daphne looked at me, one eyebrow lifting. "Who are you? His wife?"

We hadn't talked about anything like that.

"Yes," said Firoh.

Oh. I glanced up at him, noting the pleading gaze in his eyes.

"We are engaged and will be full mates soon," Firoh said. "Two parents to raise my sons."

Daphne scowled. "They're not truly yours. You signed away rights to them."

"Genetically and in my heart, they are." His sharp nod reinforced his words.

Daphne stepped back, hitting her hip hard against her shuttle. "I don't understand," she said weakly, holding up her wrist come. "The council decided. The boys belong to me."

"They belong where they'll be loved the most," I said.

"What makes you think that's not with me?" Daphne snapped, straightening. "I'm their aunt. I love them."

"We all love them," I said softly. "Don't you see?"

"There's nothing we can do but await the elders' judgment," Firoh said. "Is your shuttle large enough for you to stay inside at night until then?"

"No," she said, glancing toward it. "It's a stasis pod for three. I planned for us to sleep while we returned to Earth." She peered around. "Is there a B&B or hotel nearby? I can remain there, though know right now I want access to the boys until the decision is made." Her voice dropped. "I've missed them terribly, and I want to see them."

"I would never deny you access," Firoh said. "As for a hotel, you won't find anything like that here. Those who've settled in this colony have built their own homes and businesses, but we don't see much interstellar traffic. There's been no need for boarding houses or places that rent rooms."

"I can't sleep outside," she said.

"Of course not. We'll make room in my house. I have three bedrooms."

She nodded, her gaze on the boys. "Thank you."

I nibbled on my lower lip, unsure of what to say. He'd switched gears when he declared me his fiancée, and I assumed she'd stay in my room.

"I'll go inside and get things prepared," I said, meaning

clean out my room and make the bed fresh. Let her think I've been in Firoh's room all along.

His gaze met mine again, full of pleading. "Can we talk in a bit?" he whispered.

"Sure. I'll be in *our* room."

I went inside and got things ready. Firoh found me putting away my few belongings in one of his closets.

"I'm sorry," he said from his open bedroom door. He shut it and walked over to take me into his arms. "I shouldn't have told her we were mating."

"We kind of already are," I said with a soft laugh. I sobered too soon. "Do you want us to *pretend* we're together?"

He leaned back and his gaze met mine. His was so full of affection that any lingering doubts I might have about us flew out the window. "I don't want to pretend, Molly. I want you for always. You have every right to think about what you want from life and from me. But in my heart, I'd hoped you wanted to be with me forever."

There wasn't one bit of me that wanted to say no. "Is this your formal proposal?"

"I planned to woo you and do my best to convince you we were meant to be together."

"I think you've done an admirable job of wooing me already." I leaned into his embrace. "I want to be with you always, Firoh. I know it's sudden. After my past, I shouldn't jump right into something new. But what we have feels right when nothing else ever has. So yes, I'll be your mate, your always."

"Molly." With a groan, he lifted me up and kissed me. That's all it took to light us both aflame. He stumbled across the room, and we tumbled onto the bed, him rising over me. "I want to be with you, mate."

"Where are the boys?" I wouldn't name their aunt, though I was sure she was around somewhere.

"In their room. They promised to try to nap, though I doubt they will. We've got a few minues we can steal, don't you think?"

I tugged him down on top of me. "Firoh, I'd rather not think."

34
FIROH

Two dias later, I was cooking breakfast when Daphne walked in. The boys and Molly still slept, which meant we were alone.

"Tell me about this place," she said, sinking into a chair at the table. "Despite my better judgment, I find myself intrigued."

About the colony or Wuldron, who'd stopped by to see her yesterday? They only spoke a few minues before she pivoted away from him and stormed down to the river. He'd stared after her before turning and leaping onto the culair he'd ridden over from his place.

I poured us mugs of cavast and brought them, plus sweetener, over to the table, sitting across from her.

"What would you like to know?" I kept my tone pleasant. She hadn't made much effort to get to know me or Molly, choosing to either remain in her room or spend her time with my younglings.

It was clear they'd missed her, and that wrenched my heart sideways. No matter what the elders decided, someone was going to lose. We weren't going to separate them, each of us taking one. She lived on Earth, and I planned to remain here.

"Why did an Interstellar Interpol agent decide to come to such a remote location?" she asked.

I explained how I'd left the service after hearing from the interstellar council about my sons. That I'd followed Matis and Tatum here, then seen how wonderful it was and decided to build and settle here. "It's best for my younglings. They're growing up with fresh air, sunshine, swims in the river, and me."

"Earth's atmosphere is much better than it used to be since they installed filters across the planet." She sipped her cavast and grimaced. "Sorry. I'm more used to coffee."

"We don't have that here, I'm afraid." I could've mentioned that Matis made regular supply runs and could obtain anything I desired, including coffee, something I actually enjoyed, but why bother? She wouldn't remain here long enough for it to matter.

"You don't seem to have much here," she said. She held up her hand before I could speak. "I don't say that to insult you or anyone who's chosen to live here. I'm just used to traveling around the universe, studying flora and fauna, but living in the city in between my adventures."

So that was what she did for a job.

"What would my boys do while you travel?" I asked.

Her smile made me soften but only for a minue. I wasn't giving up my children no matter how nicely she behaved. "I plan to bring them with me. Nannies can be hired, plus teachers, if they need them. There's so much to learn from the world around us. I plan to share it with them."

"Is that what their mother would've wanted?"

She shrugged. "Probably not. She scorned my chosen profession, saying I should keep my feet on the ground. Maybe find some guy to hook up with and remain on Earth to raise a bunch of babies."

"Yet she didn't hook up, as you say, with anyone herself." That was why she'd gone to the insemination facility.

"She had someone she loved, but he died." Sorrow filled her blue eyes. "She figured she'd never meet anyone else she'd want to be with, hence connecting with what you had to offer. The boys gave her a purpose, a reason to live. They're my reason to live now."

"Don't pin that on them," I growled.

She lifted one eyebrow. "Don't growl at me."

"I apologize." I sipped my cavast, telling myself to behave. But every time I looked at her, all I saw was her taking my younglings away. "They will live their own lives. We're here to guide them and love them, not place burdens on them they don't deserve."

"I understand what you're saying, but you have to understand. They're all I have left of my sister. Our parents died when we were little, and we were raised in foster care. We had decent lives, but hardship and loss brought us closer together. Losing her gutted me." The sorrow in her eyes couldn't be denied. "When I got word she'd died, I collapsed. I couldn't imagine going on without her. Then I internally smacked myself. She wasn't gone. A part of her still lives in her sons. I need that in my life."

"Then it appears we're at an impasse." How would the elders decide?

"I guess so." She drank more of her cavast, grimacing at the flavor, before setting her half-finished cup on the table.

"Have you considered sharing custody?" If we could reach an agreement, Moonsten might consent to our decision. As much as I wanted my sons with me always, I could see they adored their aunt. It was no more fair for me to take them from her permanently than it was for her to do the same with me.

"Not really," she said. "There's nothing to keep me here, and I assume you don't want to travel around the universe following me so you can see them."

"I've had my share of travel. I'm staying here and building a life for me, Molly, and my sons. I built this home. They're getting an education from Molly. They have friends in town. Don't discount what I can offer them."

"We're not bargaining." Again, she waved her wrist com in the air. "I have the right to take them with me when I leave. If your elder decides otherwise, I'll appeal it all the way to the highest court. I've worked hard, and I've saved more credits than I could ever spend. I can afford to keep fighting this battle to the bitter end."

I flashed her a grim smile. "As can I."

She huffed and peered around at the simple kitchen I'd built with my own hands and the room in general. It might not appear sophisticated to this female, but I'd created a home. I'd given my boys security when the world had been yanked out from beneath them.

"Suppose I *was* willing to consider some sort of shared custody arrangement," she said. "How would it work? My job takes me from one universe to another. It's not like we could meet up each weekend to hand them off."

"If we felt that was what was best for the younglings, we'd find a way."

"I just can't envision that." She stood. "I'm sorry." Turning, she started toward the open doorway to the hall, but she paused and turned back. "Please don't think I'm going to come to some agreement with you, Firoh." Her sharp gaze met mine. "When I leave here after this . . . bake-off thing, the boys will fly with me."

35
MOLLY

"My turn with the boys," Daphne said from the doorway to the living area where I held my morning lessons. "Put those dashes away." Her voice came out bright and full of excitement, and she reinforced it with a clap. "Let's go have fun!"

Curron leapt to his feet and nudged his dash to the side. He scampered over to Daphne and gave her a big hug.

I loved seeing him bonding with her, but it was a double-edged blade. One side was slicing into my belly, and my worry was spilling out. In two dias, we'd go to the bake-off, and then the elders would give us their decision. I couldn't imagine a future without the boys' eager chatter. Who would I tell stories to each night?

Telsar looked my way, and sadness filled his eyes. He swallowed and rose, walking toward Daphne without much enthusiasm.

Yesterday, their father told them they should try to spend time with their aunt, though he didn't truly need to encourage them. They clearly adored her and wanted to be with her when they could. And while they knew a battle was looming that would decide who'd raise them, they appeared to be living in the moment.

That's what I needed to do. Enjoy every chance I was given to be with them.

But Telsar's emotions ran deeper. My efforts with him had paid off. He cared for me now, and I could see the upcoming decision was tearing him apart.

"What would you like to do, boys?" Daphne asked.

"We were going to go swimming in the river," I said, joining them near the doorway.

Daphne stiffened. "This is *my* time with them."

"Can Molly come?" Curron asked, his smile fading. He looked back and forth between us. "Please?"

Telsar watched us both, savvy enough to see Daphne was exerting what little control she had over the situation.

I didn't want them feeling torn between us.

"I don't need to go. I have things I can do here," I said, lifting my com. "I can finish my book!"

Curron barreled into me, wrapping his little arms around my waist. "Please, Molly? Swimming's fun. You said we'd race again."

I met her gaze, leaving the decision to her.

She forced a smile. "Of course you can come with us, Molly."

At least I didn't see anger or resentment in her gaze. In fact, the sadness in Telsar's eyes was mirrored in hers. She was savoring every secunda with them in case the elders didn't decide in her favor. I could understand wanting to be only with them.

"I was just coming to see—" Firoh stepped into the room from the hall. "Hi, Daphne." He shot me a heady smile. "Molly."

"Baji," Telsar cried, rushing to his father and hugging

him. Tipping his head back, he peered up at his dad. "We're going swimming. Me, Curron, Daphne, *and Molly*. You should come with us."

"I'd love to, but . . ." Firoh's gaze sought Daphne's.

Her sigh puffed out. "Join us," she said with forced cheer. "Let's make this a swimming party."

"I put together a picnic lunch," Firoh said. "We can bring it with us. I've tried out a new cookie recipe, and I need your opinion."

He'd made cookies each dia this week for us to sample, telling us we'd vote the day before the bake-off and decide which he'd make for the competition.

"Isn't a bake-off a silly community activity?" Daphne asked, though she didn't sound snide. Indulgent, perhaps, as if cooking and getting together with friends in town was something provincial, something well beneath her.

"Only if you don't want to have fun," Firoh said with humor that nudged aside her hint of scorn. "Perhaps you'll change your mind when you come with us?"

"I wasn't sure I was going to attend," she said. "I thought I'd show up at the end for the decision."

"Come," Curron said. "It's gonna be lots of fun."

Telsar nodded, looking between us. I wished I could tell him everything was going to be alright, that we'd come to a decision that wouldn't make him feel torn apart, but we were heading for a collision. There was no slowing the spaceship now that it was spiraling out of control.

"Alright," Daphne said with a true smile. "If you boys are going, how can I stay home all by myself?"

"Let's go get our suits on," Firoh said. "We can meet out back in, say, ten minues? Whoever shows up first gets to try the cookie before everyone else."

"Me, me," Curron cried.

"No, me," Telsar shouted in excitement, his distress nudged aside.

The boys bolted, and their stomps and giggles rang out on the stairs.

Telsar returned first and proudly took the cookie from Firoh's hand. "What are the brown lumps?" he asked, staring down at it.

"Chocolate," Firoh said.

"Did someone say chocolate?" Daphne asked, striding around from the front of the house. "Chocolate's just about my favorite thing in the world."

"My friend Matis brought me some on his last supply run," Firoh said. "Despite the colony's provincial location, we do have everything we might need."

She flashed him a kind smile. "That remains to be seen, doesn't it?" Her gaze fell on the cookie Telsar was biting. "I hope you made more."

Firoh laughed. "Plenty." He nudged his head to Telsar. "What do you think?"

"It's the best ever," Telsar said around a bite. "Yum!"

"I want one," Curron said sadly.

"And you'll get one soon." Firoh scooped up his son and spun around with him in his arms, Curron's laughter ringing out.

We walked down to the river, and Firoh placed his box of lunch on the shore.

"Swim first?" he asked. He wore cut off pants and no shirt, and it was all I could do to stop drooling.

"Yay," the boys cried out, racing down the bank and splashing into the water. We followed at a more sedate pace.

We splashed around, and Firoh launched the boys into the air over and over until I was tired from watching.

At one point, I spied movement upriver.

"Is that Wuldron?" Daphne asked from where she floated near me. "He's . . . interesting, isn't he?'

"I think he's cute," I said, hiding my smile. It was clear she wasn't sure how to handle her attraction, and maybe she didn't even realize that's what it was.

Wuldron stopped swimming and straightened, his upper body rising out of the water. He stared in our direction and gave us a short wave when he noted us looking.

"Why don't you go chat with him?" I said.

She blinked fast and frowned. "Why would I do that?"

"I don't know . . . Maybe to get to know him a bit better? You did say he was interesting."

She shrugged. "I suppose there's no harm in that."

Leaving me, she swam upriver, joining him. They talked, then left the water to sit on the shore.

"What do you make of that?" Firoh said from beside me. The boys splashed each other nearby, but it was clear their excitement was waning. Almost time to eat and then see if we could get them to nap. They were getting too old to rest in the afternoon, but we'd stretch it for as long as we could.

"No idea." I frowned, tilting my head. "Are blue lights flashing beneath his skin?" I had to be mistaken.

"Xilans periodically go into a period called Slaking."

"I heard something about that." A few yaros ago, a disease swept across Earth, leaving many of our men sterile. Insemination centers opened, and some alien species offered women the chance to have children, including the Xilans. And, I supposed, Firoh. "They're only fertile during their Slaking, correct?"

He nodded. "I've read when their Slaking is upon them, blue streaks rush up and down their arms. It's often triggered when they meet . . ." He shook his head. "Huh. That would create issues now, wouldn't it?"

"What?" I wasn't sure what he meant.

He put his arm around my shoulders and tugged me into his side. "What if Daphne has triggered Wuldron's slaking?"

36
FIROH

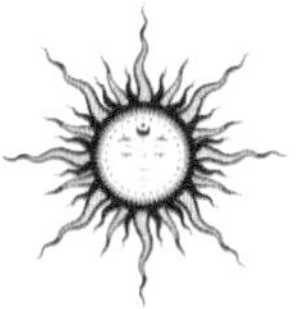

Two nights later, we strode down the hill toward town. I carried our bake-off entry, the cookies I'd made with chocolate that had been voted the best. Even Daphne agreed.

She'd been introspective since spending time with Wuldron but hadn't shared her thoughts. I supposed it didn't matter since she'd be leaving right after the elder's decision.

My fear and worry had grown over the week, though I'd done all I could to keep it hidden. I wasn't sure how I'd behave if the elders decided against me. But one thing was clear: no matter what I felt, I'd make sure my sons didn't see my emotions. I'd hug them, tell them I loved them and that I'd see them again when I could, and I'd say goodbye.

I'd done everything I could to keep them out of the conflict between me and Daphne.

She held their hands, and they skipped along, singing about frogs and princesses, something the boys enjoyed even though I wasn't sure they knew what a princess was. They must remember frogs from Earth, however. With

Telsar's interest in science and creatures, he had to have found tiny beasts outside and brought them into their home. How had their mom responded? It was sad that I'd never met her. She'd given birth and raised two amazing younglings, and I wished I could thank her.

"Oh, my, this isn't what I expected," Daphne said as we walked on the boardwalk down Main Street. She paused to peer into the closed general store. "They have clothing. And all kinds of things!"

"We're not that *provincial*," I said, hiding my smile. "We're also not very backwater."

She huffed, but her eyes gleamed when she turned them my way. "Sorry. You must know what it's like for me. Sure, I live a simple life when I'm working, but in between, I have a nice place in a city on the top of a building where I can see both the stars overhead and the lights of the world around me. It's the total opposite of when I work, and I like the contrast. I've never thought much about how others live in colonies."

"You haven't visited any?" Molly said.

"In my line of work, I don't need to." With a shake of her head, she continued down the walkway.

Villagers passed us, aiming for the community building. Some walked, their young racing around them, while others either rode culairs or in wagons hitched to one or two of the beasts.

"Freakin' dragons?" Daphne cried, reeling back against a storefront. She watched as the culairs lumbered past.

"They don't breathe fire," Molly said with a smile. "Not too much, that is."

"They're tame beasts," I said, urging Daphne to start walking again. "Kreel has a breeding pair. I'm going to select two from the next group to raise." I rubbed Curron's shoulder. "My boys said they'd help me train them and each of them is going to give their pick a name."

"*If* they remain here," Daphne said out without malice.

"If," I echoed.

We continued through town and arrived at the community building. Many had hitched their culairs out front and were streaming inside carrying dishes to enter in the bake-off. Others arrived empty-handed, here only to enjoy the fun.

Kreel and Cora waited outside for us, along with Tatum and Matis. Wuldron stood with them.

He only had eyes for Daphne, and though he wore sleeves over his arms, I swore I saw slaking markings flaring beneath the skin on his wrists. Poor guy. The Xilans had lost many of their females, and when a slaking was upon a male, most would have to deal with it alone.

Tatum took in my plate loaded with cookies. "I told you we should've made something," she said to Matis.

"No need to," he said, flashing me a smile. "I plan to eat all of Firoh's, and I'll be happy to share one with you."

She pouted, but her eyes sparkled. "One, huh?" She grabbed his arm, tugging him inside. "Come on, everyone. Let's go grab a table."

Wuldron followed them inside.

"Can we go play with the other younglings?" Telsar asked with Curron nodding eagerly.

"Yes, but behave," I said.

They bolted inside, their giggles ringing out. Soon, excited chatter echoed from them and their friends.

"You let them run free like that?" Daphne asked in amazement.

"They're safe here," I said. "No one will harm them, and everyone looks out for each other."

Inside, we greeted more friends and joined a bunch of them at a table, me and Molly sitting beside Cora. Cora held Hrall on her lap, and he stared around, cooing. Kreel took a seat at the judge's table in the front of the room.

"I can't wait," Molly said, squishing her palms together. "Your cookies are amazing. I bet you'll win the top prize."

I appreciated her trying to keep my spirits up—her own, as well. She was as nervous about the elders' decision as me. "I'll take my cookies up to the platform."

She nodded, biting her lower lip. I followed her gaze to Moonsten and the other elders who'd arrived. Moonsten's gaze scanned the room, landing on Daphne, who was staring at Wuldron.

Moonsten's cackle rang out, but I couldn't see what she found funny.

Aircorn took my plate from me to set with the others on the smooth surface. "Stiff competition, my friend," he said, studying my offering. "What are these brown lumps?"

"Chocolate."

His eyes widened. "Ah, where did you get them?"

"A secret source." Others watched. Listened. I leaned close to Aircorn. "Speak with Matis and Shaede, they'll make sure you receive a hefty supply."

"I will." He pumped both my arms. "Thank you, my friend. My Breelair adores chocolate."

I returned to the table and sat with Molly. Matis sunk down onto the seat on my other side, and Tatum leaned past him to nod my way.

"Your cookies look amazing, Firoh," she said. "I just caught a peek. I can't imagine how the judges will decide."

Matis put his arm around her, and she leaned into his embrace. He curled forward to kiss her forehead before speaking with Cora sitting across from us.

Aircorn left the platform and sat with his mate. Ulorns who were not competing started divvying up the cookies, spreading them out onto multiple platters, in some cases, breaking the cookies to ensure there were enough to go around. Soon, they spread the platters throughout the room.

"Oh, yum," Molly said, her eyes wide as she gazed at all the cookies.

Telsar and Curron raced over to join us, Curron climbing onto my lap, Telsar on Molly's.

"Cookies," Curron groaned. "I love cookies."

Telsar nodded and grinned up at Molly. "Which one do you think looks the yummiest?"

"Your baji's of course," she said, shooting me a grin. She lowered her voice. "He's saved some for us at home."

"Yay." Telsar wiggled, rubbing his belly.

Wuldron crossed the room and dropped beside Daphne who sat opposite us, beside Cora.

"How are you this evening?" he asked.

"I'm fine." She stared straight ahead, her lower lip trembling. There was definitely something between them, though I couldn't figure out what it might be.

"You didn't return my com message."

"I'm sorry." Her body slumped. "I just . . . I don't know what to say."

"Read what is in your heart."

She pivoted to face him. "That's just it. I don't know."

"Sometimes, it's hard to discern the patterns." He watched her intently, and the longing on his face hit me hard in the gut. I was sure I'd stared at Molly like this before we both realized how much we cared.

Did Daphne feel the same way, or was she biding her

time until she could leave the planet with or without the boys?

"I will say one final thing," Wuldron said. He spoke softly; I was probably the only one to hear other than Daphne. The rest spoke with each other about cookies and culairs. "Then I will back away and leave you to take the final step." He braced his fist over his hearts. "The moment I met you, something shifted inside me. As if I was crooked all this time but was now aligned."

"It's your slaking," she whispered. "It's not really me."

"And in that, you are terribly wrong." Not saying anything further, he rose and strode across the room, dropping into a seat taken over by a cluster of Ulorn females. They simpered and fluttered, chatting excitedly to him.

Daphne grumbled before wrenching her gaze away to stare down at the table.

"It is time to taste the cookies," the Ulorn running the event called out. Silence descended on the room. "As you can see, we have placed some on each table, plus that of our illustrious judges. We thought it would be fun for everyone to try the cookies but be aware that the judges will have the final say on who the winner might be."

Kreel scowled at the room. A big grump, he was one of the nicest people I knew. He'd make a fair judge.

"And begin," the Ulorn said, sweeping his arms out and bowing to the room in general.

Molly took my hand as everyone sampled the cookies. "I'm too nervous to try them."

"I feel the same."

Excitement rang out in the room as people ate.

The boys munched through a few bites before declaring they were done. They slid off our laps and ran over to join their friends.

Daphne didn't eat. She stared morosely at Wuldron who spoke animatedly with the Ulorn females. He was doing a solid job of showing her that his feelings for her were not due to the slaking. If it was only about that, I was sure one of the Ulorns would consider offering her help. They clearly enjoyed his company.

There was no happy ending here for anyone, like me with my younglings. Did she see that?

The judges finished sampling the cookies and entered their scores on their coms. Soon, a ping rang out from the Ulorn who'd made the announcement. He solemnly strode up onto the stage and stood beside the judges.

"We have a decision," he called out, and a hush fell across the room broken only by the laughter of younglings playing a game in the corner. "And the winner is . . . Aircorn!"

Aircorn leapt up, shouting while Breelair grinned up at him with pride. He strode up onto the stage. "Thank you, everyone. Each cookie was amazing, and I'm truly honored my offering was chosen." He bowed to the judges, then returned to his mate, who gave him a big kiss.

Moonsten crossed the room and stopped behind me.

Tension poured through me and sweat prickled my skin.

"If you and Daphne would attend us in the back room," she said, "we elders have come to a decision."

37
MOLLY

We followed her into the back room and took seats at a large oval table. Three elders, including Moonsten, sat on one end, their gazes sliding from me, to Firoh, to Daphne.

I was surprised to see Wuldron duck into the room and, for a moment, I thought Moonsten would ask him to leave. Instead, her gaze left him, returning to us. He closed the door, shutting out the music playing in the main room.

Moonsten's rheumy gaze met mine and then Firoh's. "This was not an easy decision for us to make."

"Hear, hear," one of the other elders, a very old male, said.

The other, a female, nodded.

"Both of you have blood bindings on your side," Moonsten said. "One of you has legal standing in addition to a blood binding, however, and that must play a role in this decision. That is why—"

Daphne cleared her throat and staggered to her feet. "May I speak?"

Moonsten blinked a few times. "Of course."

"Thank you." Daphne pinched her eyes closed for a moment before opening them again. Tears shimmered there. "I came here expecting to find my nephews desperate to see me. They love me, and it's clear they missed me. But instead of a male who had claimed them because he was given almost no other choice, one who, perhaps, didn't even care if they existed, I found a kind person raising them the best he can. He's also very much in love with an Earth woman."

I sucked in my breath and sniffed, watching Daphne. My hand clinging to Firoh's beneath the table sweated, and I tightened our grip.

"He—no, they—have created a home here for Telsar and Curron," Daphne said. "Honestly, I never thought I'd spend much time in a colony without a city or hovervehicle in sight. This is a wonderful place for any child to grow up. Since my sister died . . ." She gasped in breaths and tears trickled down her face. "Since she died, my only goal has been to raise my nephews, to show them the love of family. But I see now that they have that already. Not only that, but they also have the love of a father *and* a woman who is the mother my sister would've chosen if she'd been given a chance."

Silence rang out while she wiped her eyes and composed herself.

"What are you saying, little one?" Moonsten asked kindly.

"I'm relinquishing my claim to Telsar and Curron," Daphne called out in a strong voice. "I'm ceding all custody rights to Firoh and Molly."

Firoh's lungs heaved with emotion. "You can see them

whenever you'd like," he croaked. "I bet they'd love to go adventuring with you sometime."

"I appreciate that, and I'd take you up on your offer, but . . ." Daphne's gaze sought Wuldron. "But if you don't mind, I want to stay here at the colony." Her hand stretched out to him. "With Wuldron."

38
FIROH

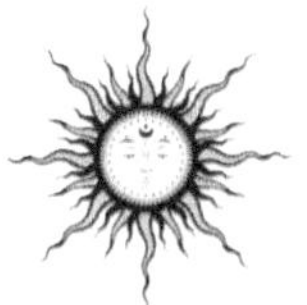

Wuldron strode across the room. He took Daphne's hand and tugged her into his arms. Cupping her face gently, he stared down into her eyes, murmuring something I couldn't hear. She nodded and sniffed. With a big grin, he lifted her off her feet and kissed her.

"Wow," Molly said, gazing at me with tears in her eyes. "I didn't expect that to happen."

"Will you tell the boys I'll see them later?" Daphne asked, her face wreathed with a smile that rivaled the one on Wuldron. "Quite a bit later, if you don't mind." Her laughter rang out.

Wuldron shifted her in his arms and strode from the room holding her close to his chest.

"Just as I suspected," Moonsten said, standing. "It was quite clear to me."

"Me, too," the male elder said.

"I didn't see it," the third elder said with a frown.

"The decision has been made," Moonsten told me and Molly. "Custody will be awarded to you and Molly. I'll make sure Daphne signs on her com." Her head tilted. "Do I hear music?" She clapped as her low chuckle rang out. "I believe it's time for some dancing, don't you, Juskaveen?" She held her hand out to the female elder, who eagerly took it.

They left the room, the other elder following.

"Well," I said.

"Congratulations," Molly said.

I kissed her and rose, holding out my hand. "Shall we join everyone else? We've got something to celebrate."

"Definitely."

We strode out into the big open room, saw that they'd pushed the tables to the side, stacked the benches on top, and cleared a space for dancing. Couples were already swaying there to the music played by a threesome in the corner.

"Would you like to dance?" I asked Molly.

"I'm wiped. If it's okay, I'd rather take our boys home and relax together there."

"You've named my thoughts exactly," I said, tugging her into my arms. I couldn't believe it was over, that I'd be raising my younglings. I suspected the elders would decide in Daphne's favor.

We took the boys home and cleaned their fangs, helping them dress in pajamas they'd brought from Earth. They barely fit, and we'd have to obtain larger sizes. It was something to ask Matis to look for on their next supply run.

With the boys in bed, Molly and I went to our room and shut the door.

We hugged for a very long time, each of us relieved it was over and with such a wonderful outcome.

"I still can't believe it," she said, leaning back in my arms to smile up at me.

"Me either."

"What do you think the elders would've decided?"

"I don't know," I said. "And I'm never going to ask."

She nodded. "Same."

"I do have one thing to ask, however," I said, my heart overflowing with love for her. She'd stood with me through this, holding my hand and giving me the support I'd needed.

Her head tilted as she watched me.

"Will you mate with me forever, love?" I croaked out. "No pretend. I want this for real."

She leaped into my open arms. "Firoh, I thought you'd never ask."

39
MOLLY
EPILOGUE

One Lunar Cycle Later

I stood behind the house with Telsar and Curron, each of us dressed in our best clothing. My gown had been a gift flown in by Tatum and picked out by Cora. I loved it so much; I cried every time I saw it.

A short distance away, Firoh stood beside an archway covered with greenery and lavender flowers.

All our friends were here to witness.

Cora and Kreel sat up front, Hrall on Kreel's lap, kicking his feet and squealing. Matis and Tatum sat beside them, both turned to grin my way. Tatum had confided yesterday she was pregnant, and I couldn't be happier for them.

Jenny and Venge had flown in with Throm and Wren, Dekrin piloting the craft with his mate, Elys, serving as his co-pilot.

It was wonderful to have all our friends gathered to

share this special day with me, Firoh, and the boys. Without Firoh, I wouldn't have met them.

When Dekrin met Forje and his mate, Kalei, at a Matchmating Soiree where they were serving as hosts, he mentioned a source for culairs. It wasn't long before Forje and Kalei arrived at the colony with their aunties to pick out a pair of pups. They were talking about buying land here and growing a home. I'd laughed at the term "growing," until she explained. I couldn't wait to see it mature. Kalei said it would look just like a mushroom and would bond with Forje. I couldn't imagine such a thing.

Shaede had offered to walk me down the short aisle, but I'd turned him down, explaining I already had someone special in mind for the task. He and his mate, Charlie, sat on the left side, smiling my way.

Even Wuldron and Daphne were here. They'd finally emerged about ten dias after disappearing together, and the love in their eyes when they gazed at each other told me it wouldn't be long before they'd be the ones doing what Firoh and I would do today.

Only one guest wasn't truly here but needed to be remembered.

I stroked the teardrop pendant I wore all the time, and my heart overflowed with joy. My daughter was with me today in spirit, and for once, that would almost be enough.

"It's time," I told her spirit softly, blinking back tears. "Love you always." Blinking fast, I swallowed my tears and lifted my voice. "Ready, boys?"

The boys stopped playing and picked up the solitary flowers they'd hold during the ceremony. They looked up at me solemnly and offered their hands.

Taking them, I sucked in a deep breath and released it

along with my sorrow. I gave each of the boys' hands a squeeze.

"I'm ready," Curron said, oh, so serious.

Telsar grinned. "We're gonna swim after, right, Molly?"

"Naturally," I said, barely holding back my laughter. Our friends had offered to stay with the boys while me and Firoh disappeared for a while. I wasn't sure where we were going for our honeymoon; Firoh said it was a surprise. A space shuttle was parked near the house, though, so I assumed we'd spend time together off planet. While I was looking forward to being alone with Firoh, I was going to miss our boys.

At my nod, the two Ulorns we'd hired played their string instruments, their lilting melody drifting through the air. The boys and I walked down between the rows of our friends, and I nodded to Moonsten sitting with Aircorn and Breelair. The latter held her newborn son, and she'd promised she'd let me cuddle him later.

The boys and I stopped when we reached Firoh.

He nodded to his sons. "Thank you, younglings," he said sweetly.

As we'd taught them yesterday and reinforced this morning, they left us at the archway and took their seats with Cora and Kreel.

"You look so beautiful," Firoh told me with tears in his eyes.

"You're incredibly handsome," I said, taking in his dark suit and the sway of his tail. He'd pulled his hair back at the nape of his neck, and a breeze caught the silver strands and splayed them out beside him. I'd massaged his leg today, because I didn't want him in pain, and he'd kissed me after so sweetly, I'd cried.

He took both my hands and smiled down at me. His voice lifted.

"Love," he whispered. "Always my love." Clearing his throat, he spoke the vows he'd prepared. We hadn't shared what we'd say, wanting to hold them close until we could give them to each other. "Be mine now, tomorrow, and each dia after that. My soul, my friend, my forever love, and linked mate. You're my stars, my favorite dish—"

Low chuckles broke out among our friends, but he didn't glance their way. His eyes were only for me.

"And my companion for the rest of my dias," he said.

"Firoh, you're going to make me cry," I said softly, for his ears alone. Then I spoke louder, sharing my vows with our friends. "There isn't anything I want more than to be by your side," I said. "To hold you, protect you, and treasure your love always. I'm yours, and you're mine, and nothing other than that will complete me."

He swept me up in his arms and kissed me to the cheers of our friends. We kept kissing as he spun me around.

When he stopped and lifted his head, we just smiled at each other. Could anything be more perfect than this dia together?

I thought not.

Until our boys rushed over to wrap their arms around us both.

Yes, now things were the way they should be.

Four lonely hearts had joined together to create a family.

Would you like to visit one more time
with Firoh & Molly?

Sign up for my newsletter, & I'll send
you a bonus scene ASAP!

What's up next?
How about monsters on Earth?
Dig in with *Candy For My Orc Boss*.
I've included chapter 1 here . . .

ABOUT THE AUTHOR

Ava Ross is a two-time *USA Today* Bestselling author of numerous titles. She fell for men with unusual features when she first watched Star Wars, where alien creatures have gone mainstream. She lives in New England with her husband (who is sadly not an alien, though he is still cute in his own way), her kids, and a few assorted pets.

SERIES BY AVA

Mail-Order Brides of Crakair

Brides of Driegon

Fated Mates of the Ferlaern Warriors

Fated Mates of the Xilan Warriors

Holiday with a Cu'zod Warrior

Galaxy Games

Alien Warrior Abandoned

Beastly Alien Boss

Bride of the Fae

A Sci-Fi Holiday Tail

Monsterville, USA

Monster on Board
(co-written with Alana Khan)

Third Galaxy on the Left

You can find her books on Amazon.

CANDY FOR MY ORC BOSS

**A new life, a new job, a new orc husband . . .
Wait, isn't he supposed to be *my boss*?**

After my ex announces his wedding to someone other than me, I'm eager to leave town. A new life and a new job are just what I need to restore my mojo. On the way to my destination, I stay the night at a hotel where edible unmentionables and a tattooed orc construction worker rock my world. I sneak out the next morning, figuring I'll never see him again.

Until I walk into my new job. That hot orc construction worker?

He's my boss.

He's eager to continue where we left off.

And those symbols on his wrists? According to orc tradition, they mean we're married.

Candy for my Orc Boss is a sweet and steamy monster romance that is part of the Monsterville, USA world. Each book is standalone, though they're best if read in order.

Get Candy NOW!

Jump into the Monsterville world!

Candy for my Orc Boss
Orc Me Baby One More Time
Gargoyles Just Want to Have Fun
Don't Go Knotting My Heart
Whose Bed Have Your Claws Been Under?
Uptown Ogre
Oops, I Elf'd it Again
My Orc-y Breaky Heart
Hold Me Closer, Fiery Phoenix
Who Let the Demon Out?
Ava on Amazon.

CHAPTER 1
CHASTITY

If only I hadn't encouraged a gorgeous orc to eat my unmentionables. Well, not exactly eat them. I asked him to lick them.

Because they were cherry.

Not my cherry—I lost that years ago. The panties were the edible cherry kind, and they never should've been taken seriously. Except . . . I invited him to do so much more than lick them, and now I was in major trouble.

Tattooed orc construction worker trouble.

Leave it to me, a woman who'd been cursed with the sweeter-than-angels name of Chastity, to get tipsy on one glass of wine. If that wasn't enough, I'd opened my birthday gag gift of edible undies (thanks, BFF since junior high school, Violet) in front of the muscular orc construction guy sitting next to me at the hotel bar.

Giggling me had channeled a boldness Chastity didn't possess. I'd waved the garment in the air and brazenly suggested someone needed to eat them.

What a major embarrassment this was. Last night? Let's just say that this was what happened when straight-laced Chastity decided to cut loose and have fun. Of course, I wouldn't have done . . . this, if I wasn't still feeling the pinch from being ditched by my now ex-boyfriend. Three months ago, he announced he was getting married—to someone other than me.

Because it hurt to see them together, I'd quit my job and taken one in a small town far from the place I grew up in. En route, I stopped for the night at a hotel and things went in a new direction from there. Tomorrow, I'd settle into an apartment. I'd start my new job two weeks after that.

I'd generated a lot of excitement with my edible undies proposition. I was popular for the first time in my life.

Two vampires offered to suck my blood through the garment at the same time, and a werewolf had taken one look, howled, and bolted from the bar. More yips erupted outside, reminding me the moon was full tonight.

The most interest came from the orc wearing worn jeans, construction boots, and a snug tee outlining his numerous muscles.

He'd urged me on because he was hot. Or I'd *been* hot. No, I hadn't been hot. I'd been determined to show the world I had worth, that guys found me attractive. My ex had ignored me for too long before his surprise engagement.

And . . . here I was, about to bail on the guy who'd given me the best night of my life. Waiting for him to wake up felt cringy. Sometime during the night, I'd reverted to being plain old Chastity.

Muted sunlight filtered around the edges of the hotel room's curtains, not quite reaching the bed. A panty-dropping, muscular tattooed arm laid across my chest. It tightened, and my orc construction worker snuggled into my side. His lips—asleep lips—spread tingles through me as they brushed from my neck to my collarbone.

Ever since mythical creatures became mainstream, I'd wondered what it would be like to date someone different from me.

Let's just say last night took things a bit further than dating.

I had to get out of here before he woke up or the morning-after conversation could prove awkward. What if I asked for his number, and he didn't want to give it to me? I liked him. I wanted to see him again. But my heart was too soft to take another rejection right now.

If I knew his full name, I could find him online. It was clear his mom had not named him Yes!, More!, or Harder!—the only things I'd been capable of screaming last night.

Heat flooded my face when I remembered how I'd shouted for him to do whatever he'd wanted with me. So unlike the times I'd been with my ex.

The orc shifted closer. He thrust his warm, buck-naked thigh upward, pinning my legs to the bed. He mumbled, his words igniting my nerve endings. The saying that orcs do it better was totally true.

His fingertips brushed across my nipple, and it responded like it hadn't had more action in one night than during the past six months combined.

My nipple was a needy thing.

Not me, though. I was prim. Proper. Rightly named Chastity.

His big rod nudged against my thigh, sending spirals of heat to the tips of my toes. Feeling its weight gave me in insatiable urge to touch it. Wrap my fingers around it. Wake him and tell him I was open to more licking.

Absolutely not. Get a grip on yourself, girl.

His tongue should be registered as a dangerous weapon. Long and thick, it was split on the tip. His highly creative tip had—

No, no, no. I needed to get out of here. I had important things to do today, things that didn't include banging hot orc construction workers for half the morning. Time was a wastin'.

Once I left this hotel room, I could slink back into my role as a respectful businesswoman who did not wear edible cherry undies, let alone ask strangers to lick them. Chew them. Rip them from her body with his tusks.

I slid out from beneath him and inched to the side of the bed. Promptly falling off the edge, I landed with a dull thud on the carpeted floor in a tangle of flushed limbs and overheated humiliation. Before my curse slipped out, I slapped my hand over my mouth and went still, listening.

He grunted but didn't move. At least he hadn't witnessed my swan dive off the bed.

Scrambling to my feet, I stood there for a second staring down at him, my heart softening at seeing his gorgeous slumbering face. The sheet had slid down to his waist, leaving his tattooed green wonderfulness exposed to my view.

Buff could be his middle name, from his washboard abs to his sculpted pecs to his chiseled-from-granite shoulders. All topped off with long black hair streaked with sunshine, a strong—now stubbly—jawline, and killer dark eyes well set in an orc-green face. It was no wonder it only took one glass of wine to make me rip off my clothing.

If I was honest with myself, something I always took pride in, he'd made me drool before I'd taken my first sip.

Snatching up my dress—a slash of conservative blue lying on the floor—my purse, and my impractical, three-inch heels I'd boldly worn the night before, I tiptoed into the bathroom and shut the door.

After flicking on the light, I glanced in the mirror, my breathing coming to a shuddering halt. Great, great, great. My cheeks were pink, I had a freakin' hickey on my neck, my breasts were perky and swollen and still called for more action, and I had a matching hickey on my upper right thigh close to where all that licking had taken place.

Lava pooled inside me at the memory, as if the hot orc construction worker was here in the tiny room with me, sliding his fingertips along my lower back. Dipping his hand between my legs. Watching me in the mirror while he did it.

"Spread your legs wider, sweetheart," he'd commanded last night. "I want to see everything."

I'd done whatever he'd asked, and I would again if he appeared and told me to bend over the vanity.

"Stop it. Get dressed. Go get your things from your room and drive away from the scene of the crime," I whispered while struggling into my sensible white panties, which I'd tucked into my purse before donning the others. Who knew where the cherry ones had wound up. Burned to a crisp by the volcanic action between us, maybe.

I tugged my dress over my head and wrangled with the back zipper, which hot guy had pulled down with his tusks last night while I sighed and urged him on. I strapped on my heels.

There. Presentable once again. Tidy enough to ride the elevator to the ground floor and walk across the hotel lobby with my head held high.

Check that thought. Leaning over the sink, I smoothed my long, brown hair, doing my best to make it appear like a guy hadn't run his fingers through it, let alone gripped it in his fist while he rode me from behind.

My knees wobbled as I fell back into that moment. A soft moan slipped from my swollen lips. There was no denying that I looked like a wanton, *wanting* woman who'd just had the best fuck of her life. Multiple fucks, that is.

Huffing, I turned away from my reflection. As wonderful as he was, it was time for me to step back into Chastity. I had a new life and job waiting for me, neither of which included a hot guy who made my chest ache after only one night.

I shut off the light, eased open the door, and squinted into the room. Nothing but soft snoring came from the mound under the covers.

I scurried across the carpet and slipped out the door, making sure it shut behind me with a barely discernable click.

Longing coursed through my veins, and it was all I could do not to turn and knock. Beg to be let back inside.

"No, Chastity," I hissed, collapsing against the wall beside the door. "You will not do anything like that."

Elevator. Room. Lobby. *Go!*

I raced down the hall.

I'd never see my hot orc construction worker again, which was just as well, because my heart couldn't take it.

Two weeks later, I dressed in a nice skirt and blouse, sedate heels, and pulled my hair up in a tight bun. I drove to my new job and sat in the parking lot staring at the single-story building.

Zahgorim Construction Company, the sign over the

front door, said. I'd taken a job as the owner's assistant. In the paperwork he sent over a month ago, he told me to have the receptionist send me down the hall on the right when I arrived. His office was at the end. He'd explain my duties then, though I had a solid idea of what was expected of me.

I would take over the management of the company Valentine's Day Picnic. I'd handle business matters not related to the hands-on construction work. And I'd complete additional tasks as assigned.

An easy position for a woman with years of administrative assistant experience under her belt.

I couldn't wait to get started.

The receptionist waved me to the hall, and I strode up to his door. At my knock, a gruff voice inside called for me to enter.

After shutting the door to the hall, I walked across an entryway and into my new boss's corner office. Pausing, I took in the expanse of windows taking up two walls with a gorgeous view of the distant mountains. Sunlight streamed through the panels, eclipsing a tall male sitting behind an enormous desk covered with various items.

He stood and strode around the desk to greet me, and I finally got a good look at his face.

My eyes widened, and I gulped, backing into the wall as I took in the hot orc construction guy I'd slept with two weeks ago.

"I . . . You . . ." The small box of candy I'd brought as a little gift slipped from my hands.

I slapped my hand over my lipstick-clad mouth, not sure what to say.

"So, you're *Chastity*," he said in the gravelly voice that had haunted me every night since I last saw—slept—with him. The deep tone alone made me wet, but the stormy look in his dark eyes made my knees knock together. "I've wondered what to call you."

He wore a black business suit, and the first few buttons of his starched white shirt were undone to show off the muscular chest I remembered licking. The glorious dark hair with natural highlights that I'd run my fingers through half the night had been pulled back and secured with a strip of leather at the back of his neck.

This was bad news. My heart couldn't take seeing him again. He *couldn't* be my new boss!

"Yes, I . . . I'm her. Chastity Jones," I mumbled. "And you're Maxon Zahgorim, my . . ." Hell, what was I supposed to call him? My one-night stand?

"Call me Max."

"I, um, sure."

Turning toward his desk, he swept his arm out, sending everything on the polished surface flying to the floor.

His dark brooding eyes shot my way as he jerked open the top few buttons of his starched white shirt. "Lay back on the desk, sweetheart."

Get Candy NOW!